HOURGLASS

Keiran Goddard

HOURGLASS

Europa
editions

Europa Editions
27 Union Square West, Suite 302
New York, NY 10003
www.europaeditions.com
info@europaeditions.com

Library of Congress Cataloging in Publication Data is available
ISBN 978-1-60945-817-1

Goddard, Keiran
Hourglass

Art direction by Emanuele Ragnisco
instagram.com/emanueleragnisco

Cover design and illustration
by Ginevra Rapisardi

Prepress by Grafica Punto Print – Rome

Printed in Canada

CONTENTS

Part One - 15

Part Two - 75

Part Three - 139

Acknowledgements - 201

Note - 203

About the Author - 205

In memory of John Goddard

The struggle is something that requires us to pay attention to both the whole and the parts, and to be ready because that last grain of sand isn't the last, but rather, the first, and that hourglass must be turned over because it contains not only today, but yesterday, and yes, you are right . . . tomorrow too.

—ZAPATISTA SUBCOMANDANTE GALEANO, "Timepieces, the Apocalypse and the Hour of the Small"

HOURGLASS

PART ONE

X

It was the past.

So you were younger.

That much I remember.

And it always felt like remembering, long before it ever happened.

It was some time before the telling really began.

Before you told me that your spelling was poor because you had learnt to read too soon.

Before you told me that you liked books *about* the books you liked more than you liked the books themselves.

Back then, everything mattered.

We watched each other across rooms.

Wary.

Amateur animals.

Eager to live but new to the craft.

Once, I texted you and told you that sometimes, especially in the mornings, I think that I am God.

You didn't reply.

I texted again and told you not to worry about it.

And then I texted again and told you that I used to have a keyring on my schoolbag that said *I am God*, and that was probably why the thought had lingered.

That time you replied and offered to make me a hot drink.

I drank it and stared out of the bedroom window, the outline of the city in the distance.

Another text:

Architecture is the art that works most slowly but most surely on the human soul!

And you replied to that too.

Because you were extremely kind.

⏳

Back then I was not good at sleeping and I disliked drinking outdoors, even during summer.

The year you arrived I had been shrinking myself.

Eating mostly apples and bran flakes.

I was happy that my clothes fit but less happy that my ankles felt strange and that I couldn't read because my eyes hurt.

I had no idea you were coming.

There was a girl who wanted to fuck me with a candle, which was fine, and there was a girl who drank half pints of Guinness two at a time, which was also fine.

I was always cold then. But I liked the smell of the city, so I would leave the window open all night and wear a brown scarf to bed.

Whole weeks never happened. But during one that did I spent an entire day drawing a picture of my kettle.

I over-egged the shading and it was ruined.

I convinced myself that stock phrases were fascist and that we all had a duty to unpetrify the language.

I once called a quite good film *a denim jacket made of fleece* and felt immediately embarrassed.

In the end, things always seem inevitable.

But I honestly had no idea you were coming.

⋈

That year I also spent some time relearning how to do simple maths I was taught in school.

Things seemed considerably harder from a distance.

One day I figured out the volume of a tennis ball that was sitting in the corner of my room and pinned my workings to the fridge.

More often than not, I'd sleep on the sofa.

It was next to the biggest window in the flat so that way I got woken up by the light of the sun and by the sound of the man who handed out free newspapers.

I liked to look at the floor in the kitchen. It was stained in a way that was interesting to me.

Once I thought the stains looked exactly like something in particular, but I forgot what it was and could never recover the image.

The girl who liked to fuck me with a candle (which was fine) eventually decided that she didn't want to spend any more time with me.

That was also fine.

She told me that she didn't want to spend any more time with me while we sat in a café she liked to go to because it had nice bread.

I could never figure out if the bread was actually nice or if it was just warm.

Your eyes used to be quite shiny and now it looks like you've always got some sort of eye ache, she said.

I was very hungry from only eating apples and bran flakes in order to shrink myself so I didn't leave when she did.

I didn't follow her and I never saw her again.

I stayed and ate more of the nice warm bread that might have only been nice because it was also warm.

I used to have a fish. But it died.

I found it nestled near the drawbridge of the ornamental castle in the corner of the tank.

I took a picture of the dead fish and texted it to the girl who drank half pints of Guinness two at a time.

The fish is dead. But in heroic circumstances. I hope when I die it is also because I am trying to breach the walls of a castle.

I don't think she replied.

Quite soon after that she told me that she didn't think she could love me.

We were in my flat when she said it, we had just had sex and her body was curled around mine.

She cried for quite a long time but stopped crying for a second to tell me not to touch her hair.

After she had stopped crying, and was sure I wasn't going to touch her hair, she fell asleep.

I remember a pale blue vein on the side of her face, like a small river running from her ear to her chin.

It looked the way tear marks should look, but don't.

I tried to imagine that her face was an important graph and that the vein said something vital about the banks.

I was thinking a lot about graphs back then.

Around that time I wrote an essay that nobody published about how sometimes the lines on a human hand look like the lines on a graph and isn't economics all just palm reading really, eh?

I saw the girl who drank half pints of Guinness two at a time and had a pale blue vein on the side of her face once more after the day when she cried and slept and told me not to touch her hair.

I saw her cross the road and go into a shop that sold stationery.

Three nights a week I worked for a large bookshop that has long since closed down. My hours were 10 P.M. until 1 A.M.

I was glad when I got the job, but had expected to work in the shop during the day when it was actually open.

Instead, I spent the nights unloading boxes of books from delivery pallets and carrying them up from the loading bay to the shop floor.

At least I think they were boxes of books.

We were not allowed to open the boxes.

I had a colleague called Steve, who never really spoke to me. He never spoke to the delivery drivers either so after a few shifts I didn't take his silence personally.

Because we didn't know for sure if the boxes had books in them I would sometimes say to Steve:

A few more pallets of Schrödinger's books, eh, Steve?

I think I knew that the joke only barely made sense, and was also not funny.

But you must understand, there were times when I got extremely lonely.

Carrying the boxes of what were probably, on balance, books used to leave pale red marks on my forearms that would burn when I was in the shower.

The marks reminded me of being a kid.

We were poor so sometimes my mom would water down canned tomato soup.

It makes it go further and it is too fucking strong to start with, she'd say.

Just to be clear, I am saying that the marks from the boxes were the same colour as the watered-down soup.

A few months into the job, without warning, Steve started listening to talk radio while we worked.

I'd get so tired that the voices would just move through me, without registering as meaning anything at all.

Sometimes, after I had got home and taken a shower and the water had stung the marks on my forearms and I had thought about the watered-down soup and got into bed, the talk-radio voices would swell back up again.

But this time I could hear them.

They would murmur me to sleep by saying words like *practical* and *common sense* and *paedophile.*

I think I heard your voice sometimes too.

But that can't be right.

⧖

Back then, I sometimes had ideas.

And I wrote them down in essays.

I sent them to magazines that cost fifteen pounds to buy and seemed to be released both hardly ever and also completely at random.

I always used an exclamation mark in the titles of my essays, because I hoped it showed editors that I had a sense of humour.

People Bloody Love Astrology Right Now Because They Fear We Have Funnelled the Entirety of Our Collective Divinatory Power into Predictive Algorithms!
(824 words)

Minimalism Will Always Be a Profitable Aesthetic Because It Allows Those Without Taste or Discernment to Have Their Empty Minds Sold Back to Them as Refinement, LOL!
(2,261 words)

Why Expensive Biscuits Are Always in Vertical Rather Than Horizontal Packets and What That Tells Us About Rentierism!
(1,811 words)

What Does Remembering Mean in a World That Never Forgets?!
(87 words)

I'd write these things in the afternoon. I still have hunched shoulders because of it.

I mentioned the shoulders thing to you once, years later.

You said that if an angel was wearing a jacket its wings would probably make it look like it had hunched shoulders too.

I was pleased that you said that.

Even if the same thing could be said about a harpy in a jacket.

Or about an actual man with actual hunched shoulders, in a jacket.

X

Eventually someone published one of the essays I blamed for my posture.

Maybe the Real Price of Oil Was the Friends We Made Along the Way!
(4,004 words)

It was you. You published it. You paid me seventy-five pounds and in response I spent the rest of my life loving you.

As well as paying me seventy-five pounds, you asked to meet, so we met.

It was a café, but it also sold miniature bottles of wine and standard bottles of beer. I remember being there early and peeling the label off one of the tiny bottles of white wine.

The tiny wine was too warm and also sour enough to make me think it had gone bad.

I'd got into the habit of drawing on my hand with a biro. So while I waited for you I just sat there and looked at the things I had drawn on my hand with a biro.

I had drawn a bird and some garden peas. You could tell they were garden peas and not just circles because I had also drawn a pod on my thumb.

I could never get calm in cafés. The machines were too loud and all the banging made the pop songs sound strange.

I took my mom to a café once and she said the noise made it feel like *someone was spitting actual shit in her ear.* And could we please leave.

After I had looked at the bird and the garden peas for long enough, I sang along to the pop songs and the banging.

You dropped your sunglasses as you came through the door.

The first time I ever saw you, you were bending down and picking up sunglasses.

You picked up your sunglasses and I was in pieces.

You told me that you had written four books and that they were all short, or maybe you said they were all slim.

Smart people call short books slim books.

The slim books were about Restoration drama, you said. You made a joke about them being both unreadable and unread.

A few weeks later I told you that you should stop telling me that joke because I had read all four of your slim books about Restoration drama.

I read them because I wanted to look for you in them.

I was foraging for you. Like I was a ridiculous chef and you were a special mushroom being foraged for by a ridiculous chef.

When you spoke it sounded like you were from wherever teenagers are supposed to be from in those 1980s karate films that are not actually about karate and are actually about not having a dad.

And also, you were the most beautiful thing I had ever seen.

Not the most beautiful person I had ever seen. The most beautiful thing.

Which is a much bigger category.

Billions of people nested among trillions and trillions of things.

We don't know how many things there are.

It's a problem.

I sometimes think that not knowing how many things there are is what makes us scared and hateful.

You said it was loud in the café and that maybe we should move.

Does it feel like someone spitting actual shit in your ear? I said, hopeful.

You said that was not how it felt.

⊠

Not just the most beautiful person I had ever seen. But also the most beautiful thing. The former being a subset of the latter, basically.

Sometimes, when I was a kid, my mom used to take us on trips. She called them outings.

And we mostly did the outings in summer.

We'd drive somewhere she thought was beautiful and we'd just sit there in the car.

We'd sit there in the car with the engine off and look at the beautiful stuff through the windscreen.

Mostly the beautiful stuff would be trees and grass.

Then we would eat our sandwiches, look at the trees and the grass, and then drive home.

We would never get out of the car. There was no need to overdo it.

That was nice, eh? Really beautiful, my mom would say.

And I would agree because it was true.

I would always want more sandwiches than we had. I was greedy for corned beef.

I am still greedy, generally. But less greedy for corned beef.

I told you all of this on that first day.

Mostly I told you about the car and the corned beef to show I had a long history of looking at beautiful things.

Credentialed. I was credentialed. I had been looking at beautiful things for ages.

That day you were wearing a blue dress.

Your hair was shorter then, and you ate two small tangerines.

X

We walked outside, where it was even noisier than it had been inside. But the noise was only temporary.

Because we were looking for a different inside that was quieter than both the current outside and the previous inside.

Also, God was following us. That much was clear.

He was just behind us when we tried another café but it was closed and He was just behind us when someone asked us for change and I said yes and stopped and opened my wallet but it turned out I didn't actually have any change and neither did you and so then we said sorry to the person who asked for change and had to carry on walking.

God was beside us when all of those things happened.

The streets that day smelt exactly the way the streets always smelt. Looking back, this seems strange.

On that day, the first day, they should have smelt of something other than car fumes and wet, sweet, dead leaves.

I couldn't stop talking:

There's a bar behind the clock tower, just a bit further along.

Every emancipatory struggle has been in some very real sense a struggle over who gets to lay claim to the ownership of time.

It's no coincidence that revolutions often involve people destroying public clocks.

Silence all of the bells until all of the bells ring for us, that sort of thing . . . you know?

You said the bar behind the clock tower would be fine.

And it was. Quieter than the outside and quieter than the previous inside too.

You held your hands together for almost the entire time. Except the times when one hand would get free and then fly up to touch the thin lines of your lips.

⧖

But on the whole, on that first day, in the bar behind the clock tower, *just a bit further along*, you seemed so still.

I was not still. I was nervous and telling myself that I should breathe the way I thought a plant breathes.

Because I believed that plants breathed in a way that was both slow and regular.

I couldn't stop talking:

Why do babies' mouths always look so sticky? Are they actually sticky or do they all just look sticky?

You responded by leaning over and kissing me and then asking if your mouth was sticky.

It was but I thought the right answer was no so I said that no your mouth was not sticky at all.

The bar looked brighter. It looked bright white. I wanted to grab all of the bright white light and pin it down somewhere for safekeeping. The way a painter cages light in a painting.

When you were in the toilet I drew a small sun on my forearm in biro instead. It went well with the bird and the garden peas and also with the pod on my thumb.

At some point, you had to leave. Back then you were a train ride away.

Give a man a fish and he will be fed for a week, but give a fish a man and he will be fed for much longer than a week!

You kissed me again and laughed a bit while you did it. Your laugh bounced against the roof of my mouth and then went straight down my throat.

I ate it. I ate your laugh.

That is how I remember it. That is how it felt.

I watched you leave in the half dark. I can still see it.

You were walking faster than everyone around you. It made me think about slaloms and then skis and then helmets and then about bank robberies.

And then I thought about the word *pratfall*. And wondered if pratfall was a word I would ever get to say out loud.

Even though I had been shrinking myself, I was still, basically, a huge and hairy person.

Much later you would say you liked that I was basically a huge and hairy person.

That you liked men who made you feel you should measure them in hands, the same way you would measure a horse.

Is there a sadder type of factory than a glue factory?

Are all factories sad places? Does it matter that glue is made to stick things back together?

You replied that there were sadder types of factories than glue factories.

And that it was silly to call glue an agent of care or to call glue liquid reparation and that also you would lose all respect for me if I even tried to mention that Japanese thing where broken pots are glued back together but the gluing back together makes them even more beautiful.

I watched you leave that first day. I was a huge and hairy man standing in thick, dumb rain.

The thick, dumb rain got thicker and dumber.

The road curved into the distance like the spine of a very old, very shit horse.

X

Before I saw you again, I had two of my teeth taken out. They hadn't made it to the surface and had stayed buried in my jaw instead.

According to some First Nation traditions, a person doesn't have a single soul, but lots and lots of souls, each of which lives in their body as if it were a tiny person.

I thought that sounded sensible, and that maybe the buried teeth were two of my collection of souls. Two of my tiny people.

But that didn't make me sad to lose them. They were horrible bastards. Horrible bastard souls. And I was glad to have them gone.

Someone once told me that their father was a dentist, and that he spent his entire life taking care of the teeth of the people in their village.

A whole life. Yanking out teeth. Polishing teeth. Scraping bits of rotten food from in between teeth.

Easing pain. Giving people laughing gas. Having a legitimate reason to tell people you had only just met that they should smile.

He had looked after animal teeth too.

And he was sure that grief would show up in the teeth. That he could tell how many times you had loved using nothing but a tiny mirror on a stick.

When he retired, nobody wanted to buy his practice from him.

So his practice closed and now people go to the next village over when they need to see a dentist.

It sounded like a good way to spend a life.

The next time your train came into the city, I was two teeth and two souls lighter.

⧗

Knowing you were coming changed the city.

Before that, I hated it. I hated it when I was a kid and I hated it even more as an adult.

It was the city where I had first grown a beard, the city where I had first been fucked with a candle and the city where I had first worried that I would spend my whole life moving boxes of what were probably books from one place to another while everyone else was asleep.

Steve, do you know what? I reckon nobody has ever blown out a candle in this city on the first attempt.

It's the kind of shithole where you have to blow the candles out over and over again.

I call it the city of tantric wishes, Steve!

I call it that because of the candles, Steve!

I bet more kittens' hearts stop in this city than any other city in the world.

And that the kittens with stopped hearts have tinier skulls than in every other city.

Thousands of little cat skulls, all over the city.

I also call it the city of a thousand little cat skulls, Steve!

I call it that because of the tiny dead kitten skulls, Steve!

I thought that one day I was going to sing Steve onto my rocks like a mermaid.

Knowing you were coming back changed the city.

And knowing you were coming back also changed the city's name.

I called it the city of the leaping train, and the city of the laurel hedge.

God lived in the laurel hedges sometimes. And if you wanted you could pick a leaf from the laurel hedge and roll it between your fingers.

God didn't mind.

Knowing you were coming back felt like expecting and remembering all at once.

⧖

On that second visit, I met you at the station.

I passed a school on the way and felt sad for all of the children who were penned in there and who wouldn't get to see you.

Waiting for your train to arrive, I came up with a new way to breathe.

If you breathe really, really loudly then it is too loud to hear your own thoughts.

You can imagine the sound of the breath is gushing water and that you are jumping off a large waterfall and instead of landing in the water you hit a rock and smash yourself into dust.

If you keep it up long enough, you can just land again and again in a dusty pile of yourself.

And the great thing about it is that the dusty pile of yourself gets bigger every time.

The bigger the pile of dust, the quieter the landing.

The first thing you said to me was something about the clothes you were wearing, and I remember that as you were speaking the darkest bits of your eyes were swallowing all of the other bits of your eyes.

We ate. And you told me you were born on an island.

That there were trees on the island that looked like frayed ribbons.

I told you I was two teeth and two souls lighter and that the difference between a knife and a dagger is that a knife is only sharp on one of its edges.

I asked you if you would push a bit of chewed-up potato into my mouth as if I were a baby bird.

I remember that you said you didn't mind. And I remember that you did it.

And I remember that it tasted like an unexpected trumpet played by a happy fat man.

X

I wondered if there were songs about people pushing chewed-up bits of potato into one another's mouths.

I liked songs very much but had never heard one about that.

The first time I kissed a girl, there was also potato involved. We kissed next to the garages and it lasted a long time.

When we first started kissing, she tasted like salt and vinegar. Sometimes a bit of potato would come loose from somewhere in her mouth and roll across my tongue.

I saw her lick the corners of the crisp packet before we started kissing.

I still lick the corners of crisp packets. It is the best part. It is where the flavour hides.

After me and the girl who tasted like salt and vinegar had kissed for a bit longer, the salt and vinegar taste started to fade.

The occasional bit of potato would still break free, but gradually they stopped tasting of anything at all.

I thought of all this that day you pushed chewed-up potato into my mouth as if I were a baby bird.

When you smiled I thought about how people talk about cracking a smile but hardly ever talk about how some smiles can crack people too.

I smiled back the best I could. But your tongue had made me a tormented puppet.

I warned you that I was so happy that we might have to stop so I could vomit in a bush or on some oxlips.

I didn't vomit in the bush in the end, but I did retch near the oxlips.

You rubbed my back and told me that data analysts have figured out that the song "Amazing Grace" gets sung over a hundred million times a year.

And that the figure didn't even include all the people who sang it to their children to get them to sleep or sang it quietly to themselves when they were sad or when they were cooking or cutting the grass.

⧗

That time, the second time you came, we went from bar to bar to bar.

It made the city feel smaller. Like a map we were folding to the size of a stamp.

We were good at that. We could have fit an entire universe inside a matchbox.

You told me that before you had started writing slim volumes, you had just hung around on the island you came from.

That one day you were so bored you pushed a safety pin through your eyebrow and it stayed there for months until it went bad and infected your skin.

Another time you took too many pills and had to get your stomach pumped. You said you licked them up off your hand like a greedy, suicidal cat.

When you said that I told you how I sometimes called the city we were in the city of a thousand little cat skulls.

But then I immediately lost my nerve and said that actually that was what my colleague Steve who hardly ever talked called it.

And that he called it that because he was obsessed with dead animals.

And that he only ever spoke when he wanted to talk about dead animals.

I don't know why I said it, but I also said that once Steve had left me a note saying that his favourite TV programmes were those really long TV programmes where people who have been on TV programmes talk about their favourite TV programmes from the past.

He never did that really.

I was the one who had left the note. Hoping it might get Steve talking. And I was the one whose favourite TV programmes were those really long TV programmes where people who have been on TV programmes talk about their favourite TV programmes from the past.

I'm sorry I didn't tell you any of this at the time.

That day you were really good at drinking. I thought that maybe you had a genius for it.

I thought that there was such thing as a genius for drinking, and that you had it.

I was there with you the whole time, but you held your glass as if you were proud and alone.

You held your glass like you were used to holding things made of glass. Like maybe you had a day job that involved kneading and rolling things.

That day you looked like somebody who used phrases like *raw materials* and *seam* and *hinge*.

I could feel my blood moving about. I thought my bones were like straws and were sucking up blood from one part of my body and then spitting it out somewhere else.

I knew that wasn't how bones worked. But that is how it felt.

I told you that was how it felt.

You told me that in some countries, after you donate blood they make you fill in a little slip with your contact details.

And then when your blood gets used, they send you a text message telling you about it.

One day you could just be putting on a shoe and then get a text message telling you that your blood is floating around in someone else's body.

There were no stars when we left the bar.

The sky looked like the inside of a cheap tent.

At my flat, I lied to you and told you I was planning to put oil on the front gate.

I had no plans to put oil on the front gate. I had never owned gate oil and I didn't know what type of shop you went to if you wanted to get gate oil.

But the gate was really noisy so I just said it. I was nervous.

I felt like a bonfire that had been put together by someone who was in a rush and who was also stupid.

As if they had put bits of rubbish in with the sticks and the sticks weren't even arranged properly.

I was the type of bonfire that burned weirdly and too fast and then someone would have to ask what the smell was and why the smoke was such a strange colour.

I put water in mugs.

Do you think the brain can really tell the difference between losing something it has had and losing something that it wanted?

I remember that you held my wrist and then guided my fingers inside you.

And that I was hungry for things that were not bran flakes or apples.

All of the things happened.

There were legs and arms and mouths and hands and opening and closing and swallowing and salt.

We made all of the shapes and we made all of the gangling angles.

I burnt weirdly and I burnt too fast.

After, I looked through the flat to feed us, but there was still only bran flakes and apples.

I put more water in mugs.

I put clean water in clean mugs.

X

All of the things happened again and again that night.

There were legs and arms and mouths and hands and opening and closing and swallowing and salt.

By the end I was less of a weird bonfire.

I remember that your skin was tight over your muscles. As if your skin was worried that your muscles were going to leave.

It was so worried that it glued itself to them. Your skin had glued itself to your muscles to stop them leaving.

I can still remember how the lace on your underwear was rough against my tongue and how your arse tasted and how I couldn't stop saying your name.

I tried to stop saying your name, but I couldn't.

There were a million names, and every one of them was your name.

I mumbled it over and over again. I mumbled your name like a rosary.

Did you know pirates wear eye patches so they can see in the dark?

They keep one eye covered so when they go down into the hull of the ship, the eye has already adjusted to the lack of light.

It saves them time and stops them bumping into things.

People think that pirates are frivolous because of the hats and the jewellery and the parrots, but actually they are efficient and practical people.

A pirate would know where to get gate oil!

You said that everyone knows where to get gate oil. And that besides, there is no such thing as gate oil. It is just oil.

There isn't specific oil made just for gates.

X

By the end of that year, you were coming to the city at least once a week.

The days you were not there were the days that my stomach was full of loud and hungry birds.

And then I would see you and the birds would go quiet, as though you had fed worms to the birds, or maybe just killed them.

Most likely you had fed worms to the birds because they were always noisy again once you had left.

Unless you were killing the birds temporarily and then resurrecting them to keep me company while you were away.

That also seemed possible. Less possible than you feeding them worms, but still possible.

You told me once where all the bird bones go. Because birds die all of the time and there are millions of birds but you hardly ever see bird bones in the street.

You knew why this was, but I have forgotten what you told me.

Every time you came you would hook your arm through mine

and while we walked back to my flat you would squeeze my fingers one by one.

We started telling each other all of the things that people who are falling in love tell one another.

I told you about how I was always drawing things on my hand in biro and how I sometimes wrote your name on my hand too.

Not the way I used to write girls' names on my hand when I was a kid, when I did it to show them that I liked them and that I wanted to touch their leg or whatever, but in a different way.

I wrote your name on my hand to try to summon you. To make you appear in the city. I wrote your name so that I might turn a corner and just see you there, doing something normal like buying water or using a cash point.

In return, you told me things too.

You told me that you felt guilty going to bars all the time and asked if we could sometimes go for dinner instead.

Someone you used to love went to so many bars that their foot fell off.

Their foot didn't fall off because they ruined it walking to bars, it fell off because they drank too much and then fell asleep on their own foot.

That same person didn't laugh when you said that the poet Ted Hughes ended every conversation he ever had by saying *Thank you for coming to my TED talk!*

I laughed though. I laughed so much I felt like *my* foot was going to fall off.

I told you that when I left work in the early hours I would always see the same cleaners waiting for the bus and how sometimes it was still so dark that it felt like the middle of the night.

I wanted to say more about how that made me feel but it was one of the things that I didn't have the right words for.

I knew what it felt like. It felt like the times that I was drawing on my hand and gripped the biro so hard that the clear plastic shattered and ended up on the floor like a special type of ice that never melted.

You said you liked to sleep in my flat because the sound of bells every hour made you feel brave.

You taught me what a sentinel was. And I liked the idea of keeping watch over things.

I'll sentinel you!

I said.

Which, I later found out, is not how you're supposed to use that word.

X

There were always rooms soaked in black light, and there was always dancing.

Before you came, I'd hated dancing, but you told me to just imagine that the whole world was collapsing and that I was in the middle of it, spinning about and throwing bricks at buildings.

After that, the dancing made sense, and I would throw the bricks for hours.

I'd imagine I was throwing them into the display windows on the high street. Brick after brick landing next to the handbags and the watches.

I'd come to hate those windows. I thought that the desires of the rich were always witless and ugly.

And you knew I thought that, because I told you. Because I told you everything.

You knew I'd love dancing if you managed to disguise it as throwing bricks.

I still think about broken glass whenever I dance.

And I still think about dancing with you whenever I see a broken brick.

If the Revolution Doesn't Have Dancing That Is Disguised as Throwing Bricks But Is Actually Just Dancing, Then It Isn't My Revolution!
(2,307 words)

In the mornings, I would stay in bed and watch you brush your oil spill of slick, wet hair.

You would leave balls of it on the carpet and I'd find them after you were gone.

I ate one of the hair balls once. Just a small one. It tasted like you. Like the sheer fucking stun of you.

It was also hard to eat. You need water to wash down hair. Even if the hair you are eating is already wet.

I'd spend a lot of time thinking about cars. I had started to write a book called *I Fucking Hate Cars, They Are Shit!* and I was sure it would be a success.

Back then there was a trend for books with swear words in the title and it obviously had an impact on me.

Another big factor was that I genuinely really hated cars and I also thought they were shit.

I was scared of them. There were so many of them. It wasn't a good idea to be scared of something that there are millions of.

Better to be scared of caravans than of trees, but better still to be scared of castles than of caravans.

Also, whenever I had to sit in a car it felt like I had been over-taken by some sort of parasitic exoskeleton.

You were the only person I ever told about the exoskeleton issue. I thought it could be one of the best bits of the book, *I Fucking Hate Cars, They Are Shit!*

You thought that maybe it wouldn't be one of the best parts of the book and that maybe the book was taking up too much of my time and I should use my time in a different way.

I agreed with you. I agreed with you because your skin smelt of expensive fruit but not of any expensive fruit in particular. And also because I was falling in love with you.

Looking back I only started writing the book about cars because I didn't want to keep working in the loading bay with Steve.

It was a lonely job, and it made me tired and sad. The more tired I was, the scarier cars seemed.

You always called the loading bay the bookshop. And you said you didn't mind the soup marks that the boxes left on my fore-arms.

⏳

*Habit Is the Ballast that Chains the Dog to Its Vomit: Why Not
Every Hobby Has to Become a Side Hustle!*
(862 words)

I was starting to change. I knew you liked chickpeas so I got
three different varieties of chickpeas when I went to the shop.

One green tin of chickpeas, one navy blue tin of chickpeas, and
one tin of chickpeas that I thought was probably supposed to
be the colour of chickpeas.

In my head I always liked that brand best. It seemed the most
coherent. The same way tomato soup came in red cans.

At some point my downstairs neighbour died and for weeks
afterwards all of my clothes felt itchy.

It got so bad that on the day of the downstairs neighbour's
funeral I cut small air holes in the armpit of my shirt and
jacket because I was worried that I would just stand there
scratching myself while people read eulogies and sang "Danny
Boy."

The air holes didn't really work and in the end I scratched
myself quite a lot that day.

But nobody really seemed to notice and you were the only person who even knew that the holes were there.

At the wake, there was dancing. There was fast dancing and then there was slow dancing.

And then there was the dance when you put your head on my shoulder and pushed one of your fingers through the air hole in my jacket.

And once you were through, you searched around and found the air hole in my shirt as well.

Your finger was in my armpit. And there was dancing.

And God was there.

He'd followed us from his house to the community centre . . . where there was dancing.

⧖

For two weeks I went swimming every day. But then something happened and I never went again.

I told you I stopped going because I wanted to try running instead. But actually I stopped going because of something else.

There was a kid there, at the pool. The kid had a shaved head and a hard, fat, shiny stomach.

I was sitting by the side of the pool and the kid told me that chlorine in pools only had a smell when it was mixed with piss.

I told the fat kid with the shaved head that I didn't know if that was true but thanks for telling me anyway.

I had been reading a lot about the history of guillotines.

I'd abandoned the project about hating cars and was thinking about writing a book of guillotine anecdotes from around the world.

Anyway, when I next saw the kid at the vending machine I wanted to give him something in exchange for his piss fact.

So I showed him a picture of the last time a guillotine was used in France.

It was a colour picture, because the French were still using guillotines right up until the late 1970s.

Because he was the type of kid who talked to strangers about piss, I assumed he was also the type of kid who would like to see a picture of somebody without their head.

But it turned out he wasn't.

He didn't feel the same about guillotines as he did about piss.

The receptionist asked that I didn't come back to the swimming pool ever again.

I remember the heavy rain as I left the leisure centre.

I remember not minding. I was changing. And the world was starting all over again.

⧗

Before I met you, I used to imagine how empty the world would be once we'd finally ruined it.

It was a good thought. And I used it to help me sleep.

No people, just trees and frogs and rabbits and fish. Maybe some sheep and horses and lions.

But then you told me that if we really do ruin everything, we'll take all the trees and the frogs and the rabbits and the fish with us, along with the sheep and the horses and the lions.

I knew you were right when you said that. But hearing it was confusing in the way that it is confusing when you eat a potato and the potato tastes of flour and not of potato.

You knew that we would be consumed by either fire, or fire.

There were entire days when it seemed like everything you said was a premonition.

And you were teaching me that most important choices weren't really choices at all.

Looking back now, I can see that there was a freedom growing inside of me.

But at the time it just felt like a man with a giant hand was punching me in the chest over and over again.

I kept old keys and buttons and bits of thread in a dented biscuit tin on my windowsill.

And sometimes I would look at the dented biscuit tin and think *That is my chest, my chest is a dented biscuit tin and it is dented because a man with a giant hand has punched it over and over again.*

But I was wrong about that. Like I said, it was actually a sort of freedom that was growing in me.

⧗

We had a party in my flat. I had four friends, and all four of them came.

It was the wettest day for decades and we both worried that people wouldn't come.

But people came and they piled their wet coats at the foot of my bed because I didn't have anywhere to hang them.

I drank too much and told you that most of all you reminded me of a paper lantern.

When you asked why you reminded me of a paper lantern and I explained it, it soon became clear that I didn't actually know what a paper lantern was.

I had got it confused with something else. With the things that you light and then let go like miniature hot air balloons.

Later, it also became clear that I didn't know how candles worked.

I thought it was the flame that melted the wax.

Someone at the party was really keen on candles and they explained to me that it wasn't actually the flame that melted the wax.

It felt like a night when I got a lot of things wrong but also a night when getting things wrong didn't really matter.

I remember the last person leaving, and I remember you falling back on the bed because you were so tired.

The coats had left a small pool of water at the foot of the bed.

Not much, a spoonful or two maybe.

You curled your legs under your body.

And I remember that your legs looked like dolphins.

And I remember that I could not turn away.

PART TWO

⋈

You are sleeping.

The duvets and blankets are wrapped around the shoelace arch of your ribs.

Just like I do every morning, I am worrying that you might be dead.

I worry about you being dead so much that I've started to think that it is the best way to tell if you really love someone.

That's what love is: the constant worry that someone else is dead.

In my case, that someone else is you. I constantly worry that you are dead.

Your face is scrunched and serious and you are slowly filling the room with your breath.

I am glad of your breath. I have been concretely glad of your breath for the three years I have known you and abstractly glad of your breath for all of the years before that.

My mom once told me that all parents want a second child because they are secretly terrified that they will do something awful or neglectful to their first child and it will die and they'll be left with nobody to love them.

I think about that quite a lot.

I know that you'll wake up soon and that makes me happy.

I've been happy quite a lot lately, I've become the type of person who hums in shops and who doesn't actually get all that annoyed when people talk about psychogeography and palimpsests when all they really mean is that they walked around for a bit.

Happiness makes you become what you hate.

But somewhere a flower is probably blooming and probably the light is viscous and slanting and all the rest of it.

And everything is leaping and everything is plunging.

And I know that you'll wake soon and that you are not dead.

And that makes me happy.

⧖

While I am waiting for you to wake up, I use my phone to look up whether bones are technically alive.

The answer is quite confusing, but on balance it seems as though they are.

I feel reassured that bone is alive and I commit that fact to memory.

Bones are living things.

I am thirsty. And because of my thirst I am drinking a cup of coffee.

Coffee is a diuretic but coffee is also wet, so coffee will do.

I'm attempting to drink the entire cup of coffee using only my fingers. It is taking an extremely long time.

Dunk, swirl, suck, dunk, repeat. Dunk, swirl, suck, dunk, repeat.

I don't mind that it is taking an extremely long time because uncommon gestures forge uncommon men.

And I've also convinced myself that drinking my coffee by slurping it off my skin is a fundamentally noble and meditative act.

Doing this is making the pads of my fingers wrinkled and stained, but I am trusting in the process for now.

The bedroom is quiet, but it is not peaceful.

I wonder about the difference between quiet and peaceful.

When you wake you tell me you dreamt that you had a tiny husband but an extremely large kitchen.

You ask me why I keep dipping my fingers into my coffee and then sucking the coffee off them.

I tell you that pressure makes diamonds and that you have woken up just in time to see something heroic.

You ask me to stop trying to drink the coffee by sucking it off my fingers and go and make you some tea.

I ask you how many sugars you want and whether you want milk. You are the only person I have ever met who has precisely no habits in this regard.

Sometimes you want milk, other times you want the tea black. Sometimes you want three sugars, other times no sugar at all.

Today you tell me that your blood feels a bit syrupy so you only want half a sugar.

I find this charming and not disgusting because we are in love and because we are in love we have caught happiness from one another like a disease.

I sometimes shout to you while I am in the kitchen making tea, but mostly you don't hear me.

If the kettle has only just started to boil and I shout quite loudly, then sometimes you do hear me, but anything after it's halfway boiled and I'm fucked.

Something has been wrong with your hearing ever since you were born.

When we are in a busy pub you have to sit to my right-hand side or you can't hear over the noise.

You can hear best of all when you are near large bodies of water.

I think this is an incredible fact about you and I find it moving.

Whenever I imagine you next to a large body of water, hearing things, you are holding a howling baby against your body.

You can hear the baby crying, obviously . . . because of the water.

⋈

I sometimes worry that I will never understand how people can possibly care about furniture.

And that at some point you will want me to care about what furniture we have in our house and I won't be able to do it.

I spend about three hours looking at pictures of bowls, but nothing happens.

At one point I think I prefer quite large bowls and quite small bowls but am indifferent to medium-sized bowls.

But that feeling soon fades.

There are glimpses of hope, but they are rare and narrow.

Once, after we have finished fucking, I tell you that I prefer chairs that don't have arms.

I prefer chairs that don't have arms, only backs.

Those stumpy little arms that chairs have remind me of the ugly shortsleeved shirts that bus drivers wear.

Not the cappedsleeve ones, they're fine. I mean the baggysleeved ones that come all the way down to the elbow.

Everyone who wears that type of shirt is always furious. Who wants a chair that reminds them of a furious bus driver?

You say that you understand what I mean and that it is quite funny but that also I should never bring up angry bus drivers immediately after sex.

I have a six-album collection of gospel music that I play all of the time.

One of the albums has a choir on it that includes a nine-year-old Sam Cooke.

Sometimes, when I am really happy, I swear I can pick out his voice among the choir, entirely distinctive even as a child.

I probably can't really hear Sam Cooke's voice among all those other, much louder, adult voices.

When I am really happy, it is like I am standing next to a large body of water and holding a howling baby next to my body.

Except the baby is nine years old. And the baby is not howling, the baby is singing.

And the baby is Sam Cooke.

There is an incident.

I trip on the stairs when I am drunk. I pull the banister off as I fall and end up breaking my wrist.

The noise wakes you up and you find me lying at the bottom of the stairs holding my hand in the air and whimpering.

You tell me that you love me, but also that I look like a pathetic cat that has been crushed by some bricks.

You joke that I am holding my hand up like I am mid-heil, and for a few weeks afterwards you call me the fascist cat, or mein Pürrher.

After a while I ask you to stop saying those things.

At first I tell you that it is because I find them offensive, but actually it is just because my wrist still hurts and I am a bit embarrassed that I broke the banister.

Eventually I buy a new banister and carry it home awkwardly through the streets. I have to stop every few minutes because my wrist still hurts and it turns out that banisters are heavier than I thought.

I have to buy the replacement banister from a man who seems really pleased that he knows about banisters and that I do not.

Thing is, I am pleased he knows about banisters too, it's the exact knowledge I need, but there is something gloating and superior about the way he lords his banister knowledge over me.

I think he laughed at my cast as well, when he thought I wasn't looking.

He looked like a toddler, a thick, meaty toddler.

I resent spending money on the banister.

The last thing I enjoyed spending money on was an ornamental letter-opener.

Two days later I spend more money on the banister situation when it turns out I don't have enough banister knowledge to figure out how to attach the new banister to the place on the wall where the old banister used to be.

⧖

My mom is refusing to buy a mobile phone because she says the government use them to track your movements.

She also says that the only people who actually need mobile phones are pimps and plumbers.

For a while I start to worry that my mom is going a bit mad, but then I realise that she has always been like this, just without the mobile phones.

I use a biro lid to scratch the itchy skin under the cast on my wrist.

I get complacent and end up getting the lid stuck in there.

At night I think I can feel my skin starting to grow over the biro lid.

I don't know if the biro lid is making a home in my body, or whether my body is eating the biro lid.

I dream about having a body that is bevelled and dented by hundreds of biro lids sitting just under my skin.

In those dreams I can sometimes see the colour of the biro lid because the skin that covers it is so thin and new.

After I have this dream three nights in a row I tell you that I have got a biro lid stuck in my cast and that I am worried my skin is growing over it.

You say that probably skin is growing over it.

That sometimes, years after terrorist events, survivors will discover bits of shrapnel rising to the surface of their body, trying to break through their skin and get free.

You said that the body sometimes takes years to properly reject things but that it always gets there in the end.

We are trying to make a home. But you are considerably better at it than I am.

I just cast around, trying different things and watching your reaction to see if you might like them.

I read that male wrens will sometimes build up to ten nests and then wait to see which one the female wren chooses.

I am a male wren.

Except instead of building nests I buy Egon Schiele prints and continually misjudge the level of pornography that you are willing to tolerate in the kitchen.

Don't worry, I'll put the one with the really prominent cunt in the bedroom instead!

It turns out that it is the cunt itself that is the problem, not the fact that the cunt is on display in the kitchen.

I find this quite surprising, but I manage to remain positive.

I buy a large brown chair and heave it into the corner of the living room.

I'm pleased when you tell me you like the large brown chair, and I like the way that you look when you curl yourself into it later that night.

You look great on that new brown chair that I chose! It makes your eyes look nice and it makes your legs look extremely strong!

You laugh and when you laugh I push your legs apart, pull you to the edge of the chair and slowly edge my tongue inside you.

The large brown chair is the nest that you have chosen.

⧖

Often I dream that we move somewhere near to the sea. We talk about it most days.

I will write a book that people actually want to read and then we will move somewhere that is so close to the sea that we get some sort of jeopardy discount on the house because there is a very real chance that we will be washed out to sea while we sleep.

Sometimes I dream that you are standing in the shallows with your back to the sea.

In the dream you are looking up at our home and covering your eyes from the sun.

When you see that I am in the window, you spread your arms out wide and I know that you are happy.

A bird lands on your arm. Just one at first, and then slowly, one after another, each of your arms becomes covered in birds.

For a second I worry that you will be frightened by this, but I catch your eye and I can see that you are still happy despite the birds.

But there are nights when the dream ends differently, where the birds come but I can tell that you are frightened.

On those nights I leave the house and run towards you, ready to kill every single bird that has dared to upset you.

But as I reach the edge of the water, I trip and fall.

The sea streams into my skull and fills every part of it with salty water.

I can feel the sea in my eye sockets and I start screaming.

Luckily, I scream so loud about the seawater in my eye sockets that it scares off all the birds.

But that version of the dream never feels like it has a happy ending.

It leaves a sadness when I wake.

Modest adventures at the edge of the land.

Salty eye sockets and just enough screaming to scare the birds.

X

God is still with us, I think.

He is there when we are walking around the city and He is there when I crawl into bed next to you and He is there when I feel the safe warm blast of your sleeping breath.

But sometimes when we are walking around the city, I still worry about things, even though it seems like God is there with us.

For example, I worry that you might be able to tell that when I was a kid I only ever really ate orange food.

I eat foods of various colours now, but I still worry that you might be able to smell the potato waffles and the fish fingers and the beans.

I worry that those smells never really leave, that they might linger on my skin like chip-pan grease.

I worry about this so much that at one point we have an argument about whether it is socially acceptable to eat a burger in the street.

I get defensive and tell you that you have a class-coded view of what food it is acceptable to be seen with in public.

You tell me that is not the reason you don't eat burgers in the street and that I should stop saying that everything is class-coded.

I agree with this in order to keep the peace, even though I do think that almost everything is class-coded and especially food and especially orange food.

A burger isn't really orange food, but a burger bun is sort of orange food and burgers often come with orange cheese on them and burger sauce is orange as well.

So I mostly feel on safe ground with the whole burger issue.

And God is still with us.

⋈

There is cold sun today. We walk for miles until the city recedes and the pavements turn to grass.

All this walking is doing something to my heart. Loosening it.

I don't work in the loading bay anymore, but the office where I go every day for eight hours leaves my chest feeling like it is full up with heavy clods of mud.

So all this walking matters. It is doing me good. Breaking up the clods and letting the mud slip out from between my ribs.

An hour goes by and we say nothing. I notice that a strand of your hair is stuck to your lip.

It stays there for about ten minutes before you finally flick it loose.

A little while later we lie on the grass and I lift your skirt up and slide my fingers inside you.

It is like the whole world is entirely elsewhere and it is also like the whole world is floating about inside us.

And I know that I love you because the person that I love has a name and that name is your name.

And because I have held that name that is also your name and weighed it against every other sound I know.

And because when I weigh that one name that is also your name against every other sound I know, my hands are never balanced.

My hands are never balanced.

Something is lifting me up and I never want to be put down.

We have neighbours now, but they do not really talk to us. You said it might be because I scowl too much and that I should get an eye test so I'm not constantly screwing up my face when I need to see things.

I tell you that I probably will do that at some point, but that I first need to spend some time adjusting to the prospect of wearing glasses again.

I used to wear them a few years back, but I never really came to terms with it. I even went through a stage of buying multiple pairs in a range of depressingly zany shapes and colours.

If I was going to have to wear glasses then maybe I'd make it a "thing." Maybe I'd become the glasses man.

You know, the glasses man. The one with all of the fucking glasses.

I didn't become glasses man in the end because deep down I really, really hated wearing glasses.

I just couldn't get over the fact that, no matter how nice the glasses were, in the end I was still walking around with bits of plastic hanging off my face.

What type of person can condone that?

Was I just supposed to accept that future, laid out before me, decades of walking about with bits of plastic hanging off my face?

It seemed unreasonable and undignified.

So in the end I gave up with the glasses entirely and now I am alienating our neighbours by scowling at them and realising that I love you so much that I might be genuinely considering getting glasses again and also wondering if maybe my eyes have got bigger and wetter since my last humiliating attempt to wear contact lenses ended in such failure that the boy in the shop wouldn't even let me take a sample pair away to try to insert at home.

I think it almost went in my eye that time, I said.

It's in my eye! I said.

It's hanging off your bottom eyelashes, he said.

And I think we should leave it there, your eyes are getting quite red and watery, he said.

⋈

Oh, and the neighbours who don't really talk to us both wear gilets. Regularly.

When I tell you that this strikes me as an important piece of information, you disagree.

But I persist.

They have no sleeves!

Where would you even wear your heart?!

Gilets are an aesthetic abomination and an affront to God!

Art thanks existence by honouring that which prefigures utopia, you know this!

We agreed on that!

In what possible way do gilets prefigure utopia?

Why are you always siding with them?!

The neighbours who wear gilets have a picture of Noah's Ark in their front window, I presume it was drawn by their child, who also wears gilets sometimes.

The drawing has three thick wavy blue lines denoting the sea, a brown boat that is a perfect half circle, a thin orange animal that I take to be a giraffe and a big rainbow that has so many colours that they have started to blend into one another like an old bruise.

That drawing always makes me feel strange. One night I tell you that I think it makes me feel strange because there are no dead animal bodies floating around in the water.

If Noah only took two of each animal then surely the flood would have killed the rest of them?

By rights, any drawing of Noah's Ark should show the sea full of dead animal carcasses, hundreds of floating emu ribcages, thousands of hippo jaws and so on, right?

I think the drawing makes me feel strange because it reminds me of death and all the ways that we hide it.

You disagree. You tell me that the drawing makes you think about how nice it might be to have a child. One who draws boats as half circles and gets too excited with the colours when they are drawing a rainbow.

Something new takes root in me when you say that. I can feel it spreading through my forearms.

⋈

There are days when all of the good voices go quiet and I don't know what to say to you.

On days like that I tell you stories about how I fell in love with you by accident and how sometimes I imagine what it would have been like to know you as a kid.

And how sometimes I get angry about all of the years I spent not knowing you and how I try to replace the missing memories by imagining you pulling faces in holiday camps and buying yoyos and smelling of sweat and sun cream.

On the days like this, days when all of the good voices have gone quiet, none of my jokes work.

On days like this, none of my jokes work and you don't laugh or smile and if it goes on too long I start to panic and wonder if maybe I am a fucking idiot or, even worse, whether sometimes you might be a bit cruel.

I try to talk to you about *The Flintstones*, and how strange and depressing it is that we made a cartoon set in 10,000 BC but still couldn't imagine our way past a nuclear family arguing about domestic labour.

But you make it clear that you don't find that very interesting.

So I talk to you about *The Jetsons*, and how strange and depressing it is that we made a cartoon set a hundred years in the future but still couldn't imagine our way past a nuclear family arguing about domestic labour.

But you make it clear that you don't find that very interesting either.

There aren't many days like this, but when they do happen I start to panic and wonder if maybe I am a fucking idiot, or, even worse, whether sometimes you might be a bit cruel.

X

I say the word "labour" more than anybody else I know.

I can't stop bloody banging on about labour.

Mostly this is because I think that all wage labour is coercive and I am angry that we have to do it at all.

In my view even the people who are lucky enough to choose the particular *way* in which they are coerced by work are still being coerced.

Because if they don't work then they die.

And if someone gives you the choice of either doing something or dying, then that isn't really much of a choice at all, is it?

I know you can choose to not work and claim benefits instead, but anyone who doesn't think claiming benefits is also a type of work hasn't ever really claimed benefits.

I've done it once or twice and it is definitely work.

It's a really shit admin job, basically.

One where your shit admin task involves sitting opposite people who have a different type of shit admin job while they patronise you and make you feel ashamed.

But beyond hating work generally, I also hate my work specifically.

I have never told you, but I sometimes cry on the bus in the mornings.

And other times, when you think I am crying because I've found a film or a piece of music moving, I am actually just crying because I hate my job so much.

I once made the mistake of mentioning to my supervisor that I thought all work was fundamentally coercive.

I was drunk when I told him that.

And I was wearing a paper Christmas hat.

He didn't agree with me at all.

He said I should use the Christmas break to think about my work ethic.

Look, Jerry! I said.

It's not that I don't have a work ethic!

It's that I think that the very idea of a work ethic is a quasi-theological injunction historically leveraged against the working class in order to drive labour intensification on behalf of capital!

Ask yourself, Jerry, do you pity the idle rich?

Jerry, be honest with me, do you worry for the state of their unoccupied, workless souls?

You tell me that in the year before we met you'd started biting your nails so much that they would bleed.

That you'd bite them down past the quick so the exposed skin stung enough to keep you awake.

And how the first time we went to bed you were scared that when I sucked the wetness from your fingers I would think the nails were stubby and broken.

It annoyed you that I thought you were shy about the wetness when in fact you were only shy about the nails.

It took you all this time to tell me that.

When you do finally tell me I am sitting across from you in the pub near our flat.

As soon as you tell me, the table between us immediately becomes some sort of outrageous and unconscionable object that exists solely to thwart my desire to suck your fingers in public.

I just lumber across the table and knock over a bottle of vinegar and a wine menu.

Undaunted, I stick two of your fingers in my mouth.

They taste like cheese and onion crisps and are completely delicious.

We are both embarrassed and both happy.

Because you tell me about the fingernails, I tell you that in the year before we met I also had a habit that I'd been keeping from you all this time.

How the first time you'd come to my flat, you'd asked me why I didn't have any saucepans and I lied and told you it was because I'd lent them to a friend who needed them for a dinner party.

Whereas actually I'd got into the habit of not washing my pans and letting the burnt remnants that were stuck to the bottom become a sort of ongoing stock for the following meal.

I'd just reheat the dirty pan and let whatever was caked to the bottom thicken and flavour whatever I was cooking.

Usually it just added a brown sauce sort of taste.

In the year before we met, everything I ate tasted of brown sauce.

I'd hidden the saucepans in a suitcase under my bed and then thrown them out once you had left.

⧖

The first time I take you to meet my mom I am scared you will see something in her that will make you hate me.

I feel guilty for thinking that, but when I tell you about it you say that I worry too much, especially about my mom.

I think I worry about her because she was ill so often when I was growing up.

There were always the same signs. She would start to vacuum all of the time, and get furious whenever anyone walked on a piece of carpet she had recently cleaned.

And then she'd start doing jigsaws. Thousands of pieces just to make terrible pictures of tigers or parrots or of rivers running through the middle of capital cities.

When she'd done enough jigsaws she would go to bed. Sometimes for a week and sometimes for much longer than that.

I'd bring her cigarettes and sandwiches and ask her if she wanted me to open the curtains.

But when you meet, it is fine.

My mom talks to you for a long time about power showers, and how much she hates them.

I'd rip mine off the fucking wall if I could, but I'm so angry about it I worry I'd pull out all the copper piping and flood the whole fucking house!

You also talk about planets and how many of them we'd need if we wanted to keep consuming at the same rate we do now.

You disagree about the number. You say four and my mom says . . . *four? We'd need over a hundred planets, not four.*

But even that is fine. Everything is fine.

Later that night you tell me that my mom is a revolutionary pessimist. It makes me really happy when you say that.

Everything is fine.

Ⅹ

In time, I start to like to watch you speaking to my mom, I like the way you calm her down and I like the way she is so kind to you in return.

My mom says you are good at "gentling" people. And she is right about that.

It is the first time I've ever heard the word "gentling," and it seems like an odd word for my mom to choose.

But it is the exactly right word.

Gentling.

When we visit my mom she won't let us in the house until we have put our mobile phones in her Faraday bag.

The Faraday bag is a small black pouch she keeps by the door that blocks out all electromagnetic signals.

I get annoyed and tell her she is being stupid, but you just say that it might be nice not to have our phones for a couple of hours.

You ask my mom how the Faraday bag works and you listen patiently while she makes up her extremely long answer.

You listen patiently even though I know full well you know how a Faraday bag works because you once told me about Faraday bags and Faraday cages in the pub.

On the way home I make a joke about my mom having a tin-foil bum-bag and you tell me not to be cruel.

You tell me that throughout history industrial technology has often been forced on people with little regard for the effects on their health or wellbeing.

I know that you are right about that.

And I know that you are kind and I know that I have been gentled.

⋈

A hot summer day. A day when the light lasts and lasts and lasts.

The type of day that is so beautiful that it is impossible not to worry about whether it is only so hot because the climate is totally fucked and we are all going to die.

The Climate Crisis Has Taken That Most Banal Conversational Topic—the Weather—and Injected It With a Constant Undercurrent of Looming Existential Dread, LOL!
(787 words)

Pollution Has a Significantly Deleterious Effect on Cognitive Function, So the Worse the Environment Gets, the Less Likely We Are to Have the Brains to Figure Out a Solution, LOL!
(3,654 words)

A day to move from bar to bar, always lagging a foot behind your well-fed, long-legged friends.

Where no words come out sour, where words tumble out like a commotion of wings.

A day of watching you take up space in small, plain rooms and of watching you pick up objects and put them down again.

A day when you tell me that mixing red, blue and green makes white, so white must be a colour after all.

The type of day that if you weren't in love might feel like the end of something but instead manages to feel like a clean beginning.

A day during which I become utterly convinced that heaven is blue.

Not gold, blue.

I've got no evidence for that, but I don't think I've ever been so sure of anything in my entire life.

What if the Streets of the Holy Kingdom Were Not Pure Gold?
What if They Were Blue? Eh? Then What?!
(20 words)

⋈

Other days have less light. Other days have less light and the light they do have doesn't last nearly as long.

I wonder if it is possible to learn to love the rain, or love the darkness, or the wind.

If we ever have a child I will take it out in the rain and say things like: *What a wonderful rainy day!*

Or I'll wake it gently in the mornings by saying things like: *Wake up, you don't want to oversleep on a day that is so gloriously humid and sweaty!*

That way it won't spend half of its life slightly disappointed about the weather, like I do.

Days when it is dark by the time I leave the office, and days when I stay out and you are sleeping by the time I get home.

I fold back the covers and slide into the bed next to you, listening as your deep breaths slip now and then into snores.

And how did I get exactly here, exactly now, feeling drunk and feeling alone and feeling like I want to roll you over in the hope that it might stop you snoring?

And how did I get exactly here, exactly now, feeling pitiful and prideful and like maybe I wasted my youth and my talent or that maybe I never had any youth or any talent to waste?

I am worried that I might start to understand the reason my mom is so lonely.

And the reason she sometimes looks like she is made out of warped wood.

I am drunk and I am worried that things might keep getting colder.

We are fighting about mangoes. You can't understand why I make such a fuss about them when they are obviously really tasty.

Which is fair enough. Mangoes are tasty. But it doesn't stop me fucking hating them.

I can't stand the sight of them and I refuse to have them in the house.

I'm not unreasonable about it, though. After some discussion I relent and agree that mango-flavoured things are allowed to darken our door.

A mango yoghurt is fine, for example. As is mango chutney.

I hate mangoes because between the ages of thirteen and fifteen I spent every weekend selling boxes of mangoes at a fruit and veg market.

I'd get picked up at 4 A.M. and we'd drive to a wholesaler to load the van. During the winter it was so cold that it would hurt to grip the corner of the mango boxes.

I'd spend all day selling boxes of mangoes. It cost six pounds for a box, and for every box I sold I got to keep one pound.

On a good day, I would make about twenty pounds, which seemed a lot of money for the first few months, but soon started to feel like not very much money at all.

People always wanted to buy single mangoes, or two mangoes, and they would often be baffled when I explained that I could only sell them by the box.

I didn't really understand why I could only sell them by the box, either. Maybe it just made dividing the money up a bit easier.

Every thirty seconds I'd shout, *Get your mangoes, six quid a box, lovely mangoes, six quid a box!*

I'd come home with bits of mango under my nails from when we chucked the shit ones away at the end of the day.

Anyway, fuck mangoes. I fucking hate them.

And I also fucking hate that we are fighting about mangoes.

After I stopped working on the mango stall I got a job in a factory that made taps.

Except the factory didn't really make the taps, it just imported the taps, dismantled the taps, reassembled the taps and then put the taps in different boxes.

This process meant that they could sell the reassembled taps as "British" taps and I think it also made them eligible for some kind of enterprise tax relief or something.

There was no real system in the factory, everyone just spent all day walking to one end of the factory to collect a box of taps from a massive pile, taking them back to their bench, dismantling and reassembling them and then taking the reassembled taps to the other end of the factory and adding them to a different pile.

After a while I realised I could just carry an empty box around all day, back and forth from my bench every ten minutes or so.

I thought this would make the day go faster, and it meant my hands wouldn't hurt from unscrewing the washers on the taps.

It didn't make the days go faster. The days went extremely slowly.

In fact, if you've ever wondered what it would be like to disrupt the space–time continuum, consider spending eight hours a day carrying an empty cardboard box around and pretending it has some taps in it.

Time does not fly.

There was one woman in the whole factory. She wore incredibly sweet perfume, and by the end of the day it would be mixed with the smell of cigarette smoke and sweat and it would turn my stomach a bit.

I felt bad about how much I hated the way she smelled. She used to ask me to come and have a drink with her at her house after work.

She said we could have sex and afterwards I could meet her kids.

I never took her up on that offer. I always told her I was too tired to do anything after work.

Which was true, even though all I had done all day was carry around an empty box.

There was an extremely old man who worked in the factory, too. He seemed far too old to be working.

His thin hair had turned bright yellow, as had the scalp you could clearly see between the strands.

He said it turned that way because of "chemicals."

The old man with the yellow hair once saw me reading a book on my lunch break.

For about a week afterwards he called me "The Professor" . . . but it didn't really catch on.

On one occasion I wore some silver trainers to work.

After that the old man with the yellow hair called me "The Faggot Professor."

That name caught on much better.

⋈

I am watching you fall asleep, sitting up, your head rested against your fist, jolting awake every time you overbalance your skull.

I like it. I like it the same way I like it when you sleep with your head resting in the crook of your arm and the same way I like how incredibly slowly you lift your head up and look around when you wake.

I like these things even when the planes crash into buildings and I like these things when there are new wars and millions of dead and I even like these things when more and more kids start going hungry and when scurvy makes a comeback and when the lines of proud people queueing for free food get longer and longer.

I like these things even then.

I am holding your hand in the back of a taxi. I am glad we sometimes get taxis now instead of always having to get the bus.

I am less glad that the taxi is taking us to the birthday party of someone I really dislike.

He's an old friend of yours, so I try my best, but it is like talking to a barely sentient ham salad.

You know I think this about him and it annoys you. I'm sad that you think I'm cruel, but I feel unable to abandon my ham salad stance, which at this point feels like a matter of principle.

I drink through the awkwardness like a hungry ghost and near closing time I find myself telling the ham salad of a man that lobsters never die.

Isn't that amazing? They just keep growing! The fuckers!

The only thing that can kill them is if they don't have enough energy left to shed their shells!

And they end up trapped inside a shell they don't have the energy to shed!

They just get bigger and bigger until the shell crushes them!

Ham Salad is dubious about whether this is true and wants to look it up.

No point, Ham Salad!

The internet only has facts, Ham Salad!

And while this may not be factual, it is certainly true.

Truth and fact are different things entirely, Hammy!

The poetry of Keats isn't factual, but only an idiot would say it isn't true.

You call me a cunt in the taxi home. You do not hold my hand.

I tell you I might write the ultimate epic of the dispossessed.

And you tell me to please please please stop talking.

⧖

The next week is mostly penance and silence.

Broken up by one solitary handjob where you use a novel technique I am sure you've designed to hurt me a bit.

Not that I mind that, particularly.

I am holding on to the memory of what it feels like to be lovesick, of how almost every day the feelings find a new room to live in.

Always somewhere slightly deeper in the chest.

I panic in the shower that maybe we have run out of new rooms.

For days afterwards I keep reading about spores, and all of the different ways they grow and spread.

I keep reading the words *dispersal* and *survival* and panicking all over again.

I talk to you about spores so I don't have to talk to you about whether you are thinking of leaving me.

I wear my most mournful clothes, too. Just in case.

The clothes of someone who always describes light as *slanted* and says things like *I love this light! I call it the halfdark!*

I send you a text message that just says . . . *here > there > somewhere > nowhere.*

And then I get worried that I might have got the greater-than and less-than signs mixed up.

I start walking to work, remembering how loving you has changed everything.

How love snuck through the city and repainted it when we weren't paying attention.

I feel like I've got the whole of this thing balanced on my tongue like a communion wafer.

I delete an app that sends me a new Bible verse to memorise every day. Because I never memorise them. Or even read them.

And because watching the unread notifications go up also makes me panic.

⋈

A whole week when you are sick every morning and I wonder if there might be a baby.

You don't say anything, but I can't stop looking at you and wondering if there might be clusters of cells grabbing at your insides.

Or maybe a single cluster of cells. I have no real idea how those things actually happen.

For that whole week we kiss in that heavy way where the kiss is always asking for more things than the kiss could ever reasonably expect to get.

Then one night you buy us drink after drink and we leave the pub laughing and falling into one another.

It's a happy night but I am secretly sad about the cells.

That same night we talk about dogs and how you don't like them because you can feel their skulls when you stroke their heads.

And also because a lot of dogs have bony and regretful faces.

And because dog owners treat them like they are their children

even though if the owner died the dog would probably immediately eat their fingers and their ears.

I don't feel the same, but I do hate the way when you hold a
cat it can sometimes seem as though you are touching its heart
and lungs . . . so in that sense I understand.

Waiting for a taxi, we sing a song we both knew as kids.

Why are we waiting? . . . We are suffocating!

Why are we waiting? . . . We are suffocating!

I hadn't noticed what a frightening song it was until that night.

No longer young, waiting to go home, no longer wondering if
there might be a baby.

✕

There's a period of a couple of weeks when only sad things happen.

Or at the very least a period of a couple of weeks in which the sad things manage to elbow all of the less sad things out of the way.

There is an election. In the middle of the winter. People knock on doors in the pitch black and in the rain.

On the bridge near our flat, the one I walk over every day to get the bus, some people have hung a huge cloth banner that says *There Must Be More to Life Than This.*

I feel on the verge of tears every time I walk past it.

The election results end up being overwhelming.

It turns out there is not more to life than this.

The night after the election results we go to dinner with some of your friends who I don't really like at the best of times. But who now, for reasons that I can't quite pin down, but are probably something to do with the sign on the bridge, I can't abide at all.

They call flats "property," for a start.

I interrupt a conversation about the different types of furniture they are planning to buy with a theory about IKEA that I think will be a quick joke but ends up taking ages to say and at which nobody laughs.

You know, I'm completely convinced that the entire IKEA empire is an elaborate modern art project, designed to simultaneously commemorate and interrogate Sweden's relationship to the Holocaust!

Factories of studied neutrality, scattered over the globe!

Thousands of show bedrooms, empty!

Toilets and cupboards in cold grey rows. Once touched by life and now abandoned!

It's impossible not to wander around those buildings and imagine all the families who left or fled in the middle of the night!

I'm telling you, I'm calling it now!

Once the unveiling takes place, we'll look back on it as one of the most profound and effective artistic gestures in human history!

Like I said. It takes ages to say. And nobody laughs.

X

I like pop songs with big, silly choruses that make me cry on the bus.

I always have.

When I was a kid, I was worried nobody was keeping a record of the pop charts.

So every Sunday I would write down the Top 40 in a notepad, along with the last week's positions, and file it away alongside the cassette recordings I'd also make of that week's chart.

One Christmas my mom got me a special suitcase for storing all of these tapes, or what, by that point, I had started referring to as "my archive."

I was really happy with the suitcase because usually my mom would moan at me for wasting all of my pocket money on blank cassettes.

I tell you about this when we are driving to see my mom in hospital.

You've heard it all before, but you listen anyway.

We find my mom with bandaged wrists and dark circles under

her eyes. It's not the first time. It's not even the third or fourth time. But it's getting more frequent.

Mom says that she is taking it day by day, and that she'll decide if she wants to be alive tomorrow when tomorrow finally comes.

She tells us that the world has turned sick and that there is a war going on between good and evil and that we are losing and that she doesn't want to wait around to have her soul and her legs and her eyes eaten by some sort of paedophile who tracked her down by stealing her data off Facebook.

I know that she means it. And on some level, I sort of agree with her.

On the way home, we discuss whether it is moral to pay some-body to clean your house.

The idea makes me feel guilty and ashamed.

You say that you understand where I am coming from but we are living in squalor.

I promise to clean more and then later that day sneak off into town, eat thirty pounds' worth of fast food and am then sick into a bin.

I like pop songs with big, silly choruses that make me cry on the bus.

I always have.

⧓

How many times a day I want my face against your neck.

How many times a day I want the pall of your hair in my eyes and in my fingers and in my mouth.

I resolve to try to find things other than you beautiful, so I spend more time than usual standing in the road and doing things like touching leaves and thinking about what the air smells like.

It doesn't work. The same way it didn't work when I was a kid and I'd spend ages looking at a sad photograph in a history book and trying to make myself cry.

Sometimes I'd end up crying because I was sad that the sad picture from the history book didn't make me sad enough to cry, but that isn't really the same thing.

I worry that there might be something wrong with me.

How come when I hear an orchestra tune up, it makes the hair on the back of my neck stand up, but when an orchestra actually starts playing I lose all interest and start to hum pop songs to block out the sound?

The Sound of an Orchestra Tuning Up Is the Closest Music Has Ever Got to Replicating the Sound of Righteous Protest!
(74,378 words)

As well as still not really being able to find anything other than you beautiful, I am also getting fat again.

At one point you tell me that my shirt is too tight, and that there is something pornographic about it.

To try to stop myself feeling embarrassed about that, I put your feet in my mouth, three toes at a time.

At first, you seem to like it, and start to slowly touch yourself while I watch you from above, but after a minute or two you look bored and then you stop.

I get petulant and sulky and tell you that I am not a saint or a child or the palace eunuch.

Which is just about ridiculous enough to ease the tension.

Some days there is just way too much nothing to tell.

I could tell you that these days every single bird I ever see is carrying rubbish in its beak, but I know that it's not true enough.

Or I could tell you how at least once a week I have a dream where you are standing in the sea again but this time the seagulls are feeding you different types of fish by dropping them into your mouth.

But I know that's not quite true enough either.

Other things I decide not to tell you include the fact that Charles Darwin described the sound of a chimp laughing as being like "a rusty handsaw forcing its way through timber."

And that Darwin was a nephew of Josiah Wedgewood, pioneer of carpentry and crockery, so it is likely that he had some love of woodwork himself and therefore probably had a keen ear for the music of the handsaw.

And also that when he said "timber" it might well have been a pun, because Darwin was also quite musical and bloody loved a music pun.

Or that laughter is a stress response, so there is probably a music pun to be made there too.

Or that laughter emerges through the limbic system and that limbic means edge.

Like liminal.

Or going out on a limb.

And how I really want to go out on a limb, but it just seems that there is too much nothing to tell and that nothing is really quite true enough.

⋈

More and more it seems like you are always about to leave, like you are only ever a few seconds away from sticking your hand in the air and hailing a cab.

I get so worried about it that it feels like there is constantly some sort of hot, clammy hand pressed against my head.

At one point, I go to church for the first time in years.

I light a candle, put a pound in the box and then pray that you won't leave.

And then I stare at the candle for so long that it makes me feel sick and dizzy.

When I get home you joke that I look like I've been breastfed by a ghost, and I know that it is funny but I can't get my laugh out.

Every time you turn away it seems as though you are turning away because you are profoundly tired of something or other.

And I know that love is a cumulative thing and that it builds up little by little and that's why it makes people reach for words like root and sediment and other words to do with rocks and trees.

But what about the dismantling? Does that happen that way too? Because it feels like it is happening much, much faster.

And I am reaching for words like landslide and like wave and like storm.

And also, you are the most beautiful thing I have ever seen.

Not the most beautiful person I have ever seen. The most beautiful thing.

Which is a much bigger category.

And I cannot turn away.

PART THREE

X

You've been gone for five years and I do not know where you are.

I do not know where you are.

Before you, whenever I slept with someone new, I would always end up spending the whole night half awake, agitated by the feeling of being close to a sleeping body that I didn't know.

But after you left, I found I could sleep next to a strange new body pretty easily.

They seemed to have stopped agitating me, or to have stopped holding much fascination, one of the two.

I do not know where you are.

At first, this happened a lot. Every few days there was someone else.

Someone new to touch, new teeth and hands and tongues and new tastes.

I could have sworn that for months on end the entire city seemed to be filled with wet cardboard.

Everywhere I went there seemed to be piles of cardboard, slowly turning dark from the rain.

Some nights I went to bed convinced I could smell wet cardboard.

More than once, my blood thinned by cheap, acrid wine, I checked my nose and my teeth, drunkenly convinced there must have been some wet cardboard lodged somewhere.

The wet cardboard months were not good months.

The Age of Wet Cardboard also coincided with me getting a new job. It was basically the same as my old job, except it paid me £1.20 an hour more and I had to wear a tie while I sat there all day and tried not to weep.

Every morning I'd take a tie from my tie hanger. My tie hanger that at night looked like a garish waterfall of wax tongues.

I'd tie it around my neck and survey the Empire of Wet Cardboard.

Sometimes, on my way home from work, I could feel the moon mocking me, telling me that the Epoch of Wet Cardboard would never wane.

And that the sun would never come, and the cardboard would never dry.

The moon was a bastard.

⋈

I still drew on my hands. Mostly triangles or that type of 3D box that everybody learns how to draw when they are at primary school.

For a while I would write your name on my hands, half believing I could summon you again.

But God was not with us this time, even though I kept leaving space for him to appear.

Eventually, I stopped writing your name and moved on to just putting your initial in one of the triangles or in one of the boxes.

But mostly I just kept walking forward, with a sort of pedantic commitment to blankness.

Mostly, it worked, and if there was enough powder and enough wine I could blunt the fact that my skin was still utterly alive with you.

But occasionally, this tactic would falter. I'd be on the bus and then suddenly remember that I had lost you.

It always felt like I was being forced to swallow my own heart, or sometimes my own fist (it is commonly known that the heart and the fist are similar sizes but dissimilar textures).

More than once I found myself getting off before my stop, desperate for air.

Whenever that happened, I'd spend the next couple of days blundering forward in the hot spite of desire, doing really fucking stupid things.

I told a woman who asked me for the time that I had never owned a watch because they remind me too much of death.

Watches are just really shit memento mori!

I already know I'm dying, I don't need to pay for the privilege of actually watching the time tick away!

I meet a woman who has the Russian word for slut tattooed on her breast because her Russian ex-husband used to get off on loaning her out to other men and then watching them hit her over Skype.

I ask if she enjoyed that too.

She says she hated setting up the Skype thing because it felt awkward, but other than that she didn't mind it.

An hour later I have her hair tangled in my fist, and I feel something breaking in me.

I feel sad and embarrassed and I end up crying rather than fucking her.

Her ex-husband watches the whole thing happen on Skype.

Turns out they still do the Skype thing, even though they are divorced.

After a while he stops trying to masturbate and asks me if I am O.K.

The ugliest summer, the entire city boiled pink like cheap bacon.

Endless, unnumbered days. Just like the days that came before the summer, but warmer.

The same shit days, except now I am sweating.

The speed at which I bore and alienate my friends on a night out increases rapidly; at the peak of my powers I can sense them glazing over within minutes of me arriving.

I talk in long, halting blocks, and ask rhetorical questions like . . . *Surely you recognise that really distinct feeling that happens when you are doing something normal like drinking a glass of water and then you get this revelatory sense that the most beautiful part of your life has ended and that you've never been so sure about anything, ever, apart from perhaps the fact there is not a single thing you can do about it?*

And then I carry on speaking before anyone can respond.

My most patient friends might last a few hours, but eventually they'll give up and go home.

After a while, I don't mind this too much, because I've developed a technique to deal with it.

It's a three-part technique:

First, continue drinking alone until the pub closes.

Second, leave the pub.

Third, drink at home until I fall asleep.

I still write most days, but it has been some months since any-one replied to any of my ideas.

Anything Might Happen Next Week: Surprise as an Antidote to Suicidal Ideation! (204 words)

Your Boss Is a Cunt and You Are Your Own Boss: Against the Internalisation of the Entrepreneurial Mindset! (4,567 words)

You Are Not Working from Home, You Are Living at Work, You Dumb-Dumb! (1,101 words)

⧗

Without you in it, the flat starts to feel strange and I convince myself that I don't know where anything goes.

Every time I look at an object, it never seems to be in the right place.

Take a wooden spoon, for example. Where the fuck is a wooden spoon supposed to go?

I google *where to store a wooden spoon* but am met with a tsunami of conflicting information.

So in the end I throw the wooden spoon in the bin. I feel like this is the only choice I have. Which means it isn't really a choice. The wooden spoon has to go in the bin. It is what it is.

After I put the wooden spoon in the bin I feel a bit better about things. So I start to put more and more things in the bin.

I put a toaster in the bin, a spice rack in the bin, a small wooden thing full of toiletries in the bin and, lastly, I put a selection of knives and forks in the bin.

The flat still feels strange, but I think I feel a bit less worried about where everything goes, because I've realised that if I get too confused I can just throw whatever is bothering me in the bin.

In between throwing things in the bin, I mostly sleep and watch hours and hours of old pop music videos on the internet.

By the afternoons I am always screen sick, red-eyed and unable to concentrate.

And I start to eat so much that I sweat. Mostly it is cheap bread with melted cheese.

Every now and then I feel disgusted enough to break the cycle and I'll manage a few days of apples and bran flakes and praying.

But it doesn't stick. Nothing sticks.

Fascism Is Nihilism Made Public and Nihilism Is Fascism Made Private! (26 words)

I don't know where things go and I don't know where you are.

There are always low points. Every week that passes offers up something deeply shit.

Mercifully, most of the deeply shit things fade away after a few days and I never have to think about them again.

But sometimes, they are so unbelievably shit that they stick around.

One such unbelievably shit thing was the time I berated a child in a supermarket.

Or, to be more accurate: the time I berated a child in an extremely busy supermarket and then the child cried very loudly in the extremely busy supermarket.

He was in front of me in the queue, packing the last of his mother's shopping into a plastic bag and then handing it to her.

I assumed he wasn't paying attention, because as the first few items of my shop were scanned through by the hasty checkout girl, the child started packing those as well.

As soon as I noticed, I asked him to stop.

Mate, those beans don't belong to your mom's shop, they are mine, so can you put them back please?

He stuttered a bit . . . *No, erm, you don't understand . . .*

I was impatient.

I do understand mate, it's pretty simple, they are my beans so you need put them back.

Take them out of the plastic bag and put them back.

Put the beans back now!

The child tentatively took the cans of beans out of the plastic bag, welling up as he did it.

But he didn't leave, he just stood there, crying, louder and louder.

I looked at the checkout girl for support but she was looking back at me with what I can only describe as pure disgust.

He's packing bags for the Boy Scouts. If you didn't want to give him a donation, that's fine, but there was no need to shout at him.

The fucking child was still crying.

I didn't mean to shout at him, I just thought he was stealing my fucking beans, how was I supposed to know he was collecting for the Boy Scouts?

She basically spat at me . . . *Well, it says Boy Scouts on his jumper in big letters and there is one at every checkout.*

The child was still crying at that exact moment I decided to abandon my beans and leave the extremely busy supermarket.

I think about the crying child every day.

He's probably still there, crying, the sneaky bean-stealing fuck.

⋈

Days when I am fourteen again and I spend hour after hour after hour doing nothing but listening to music.

Mostly I listen to pop music from the 1970s because I like how long the songs are and how they are full of weird sounds that are clearly in there because somebody has just invented a new instrument of some sort and everybody has got excited about it.

But other times I listen to choir music, preferably sung in a language I don't understand.

I download hundreds of songs by a Bulgarian women's choir, and I am so moved by it that I don't really know what to do with myself.

I listen to so much music that I write this on the internet:

For musicians, the birth of recorded sound also heralded the birth of self-consciousness; precise, daring players were forced to recognise their own mistakes, which would now be preserved for all time . . . in response, vibrato became orthodoxy in order to mask tonal intent, so what we think of as the tremor of emotion was actually just a fear of failure!

The post gets three responses within the first minute. Two of them point out that what I have said is not true but the third one is more circumspect.

That one says . . . *Do you have a source for this? It doesn't seem quite right to me.*

I feel a bit embarrassed and end up deleting my post.

I deleted it because I didn't want to risk a repeat of that time I made a comment about how all novels published in the last decade are about water and then everybody said I was a sexist prick for reasons I never really understood but pretended to agree with in public.

Later that same night I pulled myself along the floor on my stomach like a gastropod just to see how it felt.

How much is too much? I wondered, looking at the carpet burns around my pale belly.

I look at them again the next day, angry red marks streaked across my middle.

The mirror is cruel. I stand in front of it and look at myself from every angle.

I am fat, that is undeniable. I am also almost bald. I have four grey chest hairs and my neck is unbelievably thick.

And not in that . . . *look at that strong man with his thick neck* . . . sort of way.

More, in a . . . *look at that fat, balding fuck with his unbelievably thick neck* . . . sort of way.

That's the trouble with getting old and ugly; you take your eye off the ball for a second and before you know it, it is all over.

One chink in the armour and the reaper just sneaks in and then your breastplate is riddled with rust.

As I have got uglier, I have started lying more.

I tell a woman in a bar who has really big, really beautiful hands that at any given time I only permit myself to own as many possessions as can fit in a World War Two evacuee's suitcase.

I tell her I want a simple, clean, empty life and then later I forget to be ashamed when she comes home with me and sees that it is clearly not true.

I talk to her about the Bulgarian women's choir and explain how each song is supposed to mark an important event, like a wedding, or festival, or the death of a child.

The next morning, I can remember how my fingers felt hooked under the elastic of her underwear, and how it felt to be in her mouth but not be able to get hard.

I make round after round of toast, but I am so hungry that I eat each one before it is properly toasted.

Six slices down, I am still not satisfied.

I become obsessed with running a marathon and convince myself that fitness and training are largely irrelevant and that all it really takes is a strong mind and a willingness to die.

One Sunday morning I wake up, hungover. Or at least I thought I was hungover. In retrospect, I was still drunk.

I am confident that God is with me and that this is the day I will run a marathon.

The plan is simple, I will download a GPS tracker on my phone, run thirteen miles down the main road, turn around and then run thirteen miles back, and then I will never tell anyone that I ran a marathon.

It will be a small, private triumph.

The first mistake that I make, apart from doing no training whatsoever, is that I am still drunk.

The second mistake is that I can't find a T-shirt to run in, so end up running in a jumper instead. This is so hot and such a bad idea that within two minutes of starting my marathon I have taken off the jumper and tied it around my waist.

I am running down the road, topless.

The third mistake is that I do not plan a route, so find myself running down a busy main road on a Saturday morning. It is full of horrified shoppers, some of whom look visibly appalled as I trundle past them.

The fourth mistake I make is not aborting the marathon when, after about six minutes, I have to stop in order to throw up in a bush.

Instead, I carry on for some time, until finally my ankles are hurting so much that I have to stop.

I walk slowly back to the flat, dripping in sweat and defeated.

When I check the GPS tracker I have run exactly 1.8 miles.

I collapse onto the bed and wake up five hours later, my laptop still open on my chest.

The screen is still showing the search results for the query I typed before I fell back to sleep:

Are GPS trackers always 100% accurate?

How much is too much?

⋈

After a while, things start to get a bit quieter. I try hard to make them that way.

I walk for hours every day, with no purpose whatsoever. I train myself to just get up and then start walking.

I tell people who ask how I am that I am beginning to commune with the outdoors or that I am learning to love the air or that I am taking a renewed interest in the contours of public space.

Anything to shut them up.

I stop going to work. I explain to them that I am unwell and that I need to walk for at least five hours a day in order to feel better.

This works for a few weeks, until it doesn't. Somebody from HR calls to ask me whether I am on *the road to recovery.*

I say that nothing feels good anymore, or maybe everything feels good all of time, which amounts to the same thing.

More time passes and now I go to the Jobcentre once a week instead of the office. I go so that somebody called Keith can ritually humiliate me.

The third time I go to the Jobcentre I see a woman fall over on the steps outside of the building as I'm leaving.

Her leg splits open like ripe fruit and her blood is almost black.

I ask her if she wants me to call an ambulance but she is worried about missing her appointment so she just hobbles into the building, dripping blood onto the floor.

I can tell that she is embarrassed and doesn't want me to trail after her or insist that she does something about her leg which is pissing black blood all over the place, so I just leave and hope somebody else does something about it and that she doesn't miss her appointment.

Next time I am there I ask Keith if he knows what happened to the lady with the bleeding leg, but Keith tells me he doesn't know anything about it, and anyway, they get things like that happening every day.

I really, really fucking hate Keith.

⋈

I get lucky. Something happens that means I never have to see Keith again.

I am telling an old friend about my walking habit and how I'm not sure whether everything feels good or nothing feels good and how I'm also not sure whether there is much of a difference.

Which is something I find myself saying a lot.

Either way, mate . . . I intend to spend a whole year just walking about . . . no, I don't listen to anything while I'm walking . . . no, especially not fucking podcasts . . . I just like not thinking about anything at all.

I deliberately don't tell him that I always think about you while I walk. And that more often than not I imagine that you are actually there, walking next to me.

Do you ever have those days where it seems as though there are no actual gaps between any of the buildings? Like every building is just nestled against every other building, and maybe if you knocked down one building every other building would fall as well?

My friend is patient, he explains that he has never had a day like that and that he isn't sure what I mean and that I should probably start to work a bit more and walk a bit less.

I am not at all confident that he is right about that, but when he offers me a job copywriting for a wedding magazine I say yes straight away.

It turns out to be an easy job. All I have to do is write descriptions of wedding dresses.

After the second day I don't even look at the dress before I write the description.

Every single description is a variant of the same statement.

Do you have a healthy respect for tradition but also an eye for the modern? Then this is the dress for you!

Are you drawn to a heritage look but also appreciative of an avantgarde flourish? Then this is the dress for you!

Are you the type of person who reveres the classic, but also bloody loves the contemporary? Then this is the dress for you!

As long as you didn't deviate from that formula, it was always fine.

I pitched an editorial once about how wedding rings should properly be conceived as the only socially approved kink object. A type of bondage equipment that publicly signalled the rules of one's sexual contract in the same way that a dog collar or a gimp mask might.

But it wasn't that type of magazine, really.

More of a catalogue, to be honest.

Ⅹ

I get a letter and I think it is from you. It is the handwriting on the envelope that gives it away.

There was always something about your "O"s, they looked like little children with little fucked up, bald, bumpy heads.

I carry the letter around with me for a week before I open it, taking it back and forth to work and spending a good chunk of the day staring at it.

I treat it the same way I treated the first scratchcard I ever got.

I was about fourteen and scratchcards were quite a new thing back then.

I bought one on my way home from school and refused to scratch off the silver to find out if I'd won.

I preferred to just carry it around in my pocket and imagine what I would do with all of the money.

It always seemed clear to me that it was a winning ticket, and I spent hours thinking about all of the things I could buy my mom to make her happier even though it was really hard to imagine what she would want and even though she always said she hated fancy things because they were for idiots.

On the eighth day, I open your letter and my eyes swim down the page and take in all of the marks you have made with your pen.

Your letter says that you hadn't really wanted to write to me but that there are three things you need to say.

The first is to request that I stop writing to you, that your mother has been forwarding all of the letters but that you have thrown them all away without opening them because it is easier that way.

The second is that you are fine, that you have been living in Greece for a little while because it is cheap but that you have since moved to an old mill town, which is quiet and empty.

Third, you tell me that you are getting married and that you are having a baby and that it might have already arrived by the time I get your letter and that you are happy about it but that it is also really weird to have something growing inside you.

And then the letter is over.

Do you want to know how the person you love is doing but also have a healthy distaste for the realities of the present? Then this is the letter for you!

◠
◡

It is still summer, but I always wear a coat. I wear the same coat every day, an old woollen one I have owned since the time we first met.

I have newer coats, better coats. Writing descriptions of wedding dresses I have never seen pays better than any job I have ever had. But I still prefer the old coat.

If I close my eyes and picture myself, I am always, always, wearing the old coat.

When I do this I am usually striding through the city, the streets are crowded but I am moving through them quickly, as if I have somewhere to be. As if I have anywhere to be.

I know that this is a false image, because I walk through the city every day, and I know exactly how I look.

For a start, I am doing exactly that, *walking*, there is no striding to speak of. And I don't move quickly, I sort of lumber along and there are always people in the way and occasionally we bang into one another and swear.

All summer I wear that coat, sweating and lumbering and bumping into people and swearing.

It feels as though there are fragments of something or other always floating in front of my eyes and that if I squint to try and see what they are they fall away before I can make out their shape.

I am falling to pieces, I think. My back hurts all of the time, and sometimes I am sick for no reason whatsoever.

I'd always imagined that my downfall would be grander, or more tragic, and that it would involve more invocations and spells and maybe some martyrs or a shaman.

But it is actually incredibly boring.

I still can't stop talking to people about the labour market and how all work is coercive and at one point I plant an acorn in a graveyard, like an absolute prick.

Another time, I make a shrine for you and your child and light all the small candles with a cook's match, like an absolute prick.

I want God to be with me but I'm not sure that He is.

Gods aren't flattered by prayers that you don't mean.

X

Like I said, I think I am falling apart and it is incredibly boring and nothing like the way I thought falling apart would be from having spent most of my teenage years reading books about people falling apart and listening to music about people falling apart and occasionally lying to women and saying that I was falling apart too, exactly like the people who were falling apart in the books and the songs.

My falling apart looks mostly like chasing the sun around, moving throughout the day to be as directly under it as I can possibly be.

And it also looks like occasionally asking birds questions. None of the birds answer me but some of them are polite enough to hang around for a bit and silently nod at me.

At one particular moment, my falling apart looks like me falling over, putting my hands out to stop myself and ending up shattering one of my wrists. Again.

Because I am extremely lonely and also falling apart, people think that I have deliberately hurt myself and come to visit me during the two days I spend in hospital.

When people visit me I say the same thing over and over again, I say that I am totally fine and I say that it is really nice that they have come to see me and also that I am totally fine.

There is a day when I want to write an essay about how the meaning of love is wanting someone to have the biggest, most free life, but how usually there is also a silent parenthesis attached that says something like . . . *but only if it includes me.*

There is a day when I think about shaving my head, which barely has any hair left on it anyway.

And there is a day when I think about starting to dress in a way where it isn't entirely clear if I am flamboyant or am actually wearing a costume.

In the end, I do none of those things.

Instead, I reread an old essay that I wrote.

Anything Might Happen Next Week: Surprise as An Antidote to Suicidal Ideation! (3,204 words)

The first line says:

There are living things everywhere. It hurts to realise that. And it hurts even more to say it out loud.

With hindsight, I can see why nobody wanted to publish it.

It's a bit moany, for a start.

X

A conclusion. You have to live. What else is there to do with a life?

I spend some time walking around my flat, picking up some of my ugly possessions and then putting them back down again in exactly the same place.

During this process I notice how pleasant it is to hold a pencil on its tip using only one finger and a tiny amount of pressure and wonder if this might be what loving someone properly is like.

I also spend some time phoning people up and asking them if they'd like to come to watch karaoke with me.

Eventually someone agrees, as long as I promise not to talk to him about how beautiful the word karaoke is and also promise not to cry.

The karaoke pub has two rooms, only one of which is ever open. The other one just has twenty or so plastic chairs, some orange and some blue.

In the main room there are a handful of people. Maybe ten dotted about the tables, and a couple resting their weight against the wooden bar.

I notice one of them picking off the varnish with his fingernail.

The room has a cork noticeboard that is entirely free of notices. I am quite pleased it has no notices, that way there is everything still to play for, notice-wise.

This night is the most O.K. I have felt since I got your letter.

I watch people drunkenly fight with pop songs and eventually wrangle them under control. People threaten to murder the songs, but mostly the songs blink first.

You have to live.

⧖

Because you have to live there is a night when I walk to a book-shop and then sit in the bookshop and listen to some writers read from their books.

I walk there because I am still walking everywhere. It's still way too much walking, but I am doing my absolute best to walk a little bit less every day.

It's a type of anti-training, and it's beginning to pay off. It has been weeks since I have felt the familiar wetness of blood in my shoes, which always felt nice for a few seconds until I remembered it was probably because one (or more) of my toenails had fallen off.

Each of the readings is from a book about witches, and I wish I had known that before I made the choice to leave the house.

Afterwards the writers sit in a line and have a long discussion about what it means to write books about witches.

As far as I can tell, not a single funny thing is said throughout the whole event, which goes on for about three hours.

I get a bit frightened when people talk for ages and nobody says anything funny. Always have done.

That's my problem, of course, not the problem of the humour-less writers of books about witches.

After the witch talk has ended I drink four plastic cups of warm wine one after another and then feel awkward standing on my own so attempt to join a conversation.

I ask the group how many toenails they have lost in the last month and nobody really answers me, so I slightly change tack.

The language of protest is deeply ableist, when you think about it; standing (standing!) up for what you believe in, marching (marching!) in the street . . . imagine how that must feel to peo-ple who have issues with their feet.

This goes slightly better, and I feel a bit less awkward.

I leave on a high, go home, fall asleep and then have a dream about you.

In the dream you have the head of a fish, and massive fish eyes.

I can see myself reflected in your massive fish eyes and I realise that my head is a rusty, graceless harpoon.

When I wake up the next day I decide I will try to go a whole day without walking about.

It works. I stay in bed all day.

⋈

My mom is sick. And I worry that this time is not like all the other times.

The next time I see her she looks so unwell. Like somebody has drawn her but then lost confidence in their talent and started to rub her out. Blurring all her lines.

She is unnervingly talkative.

She tells me that it is better not to think about anything because life is shit and thinking just makes you notice its shitness even more.

She tells me to be kind to people.

And then she tells me that I am right, that this time is not like all the other times:

If you hurt yourself enough then eventually your body gets the message and something bad starts growing inside you.

And then she tells me a very long, very complicated conspiracy theory that ends up being extremely racist.

I don't tell her that her theory is racist. Instead we just sit there together for a bit until it is time for me to leave.

That night I cry so much that my crying turns into a scream and then a sort of animal sound and it goes on so long that I pull a muscle in my back.

God is not with me. Not when I cry, not when I scream and not when I make animal sounds until I pull a muscle in my back. The fuck.

The next morning I go to a nearby church and stand outside. I look at the bricks and the windows because something tells me that if you stare at a church for long enough then something extraordinary will happen.

Like I might have a vision of a whole new type of blue that nobody has ever seen before and that I am sure is the colour of heaven and then I might go home and find a stone on my doorstep that is that exact same shade of blue.

Something extraordinary, like that.

Nothing extraordinary happens, but I do make the decision to start talking more quietly and more slowly so that people think I am wise.

And I also write something about my mom.

Sickness, the State and the Social Contract: Exploring the Link between Chronic Pain and the Conspiratorial Mind! (9,346 words)

X

I have got really good at writing descriptions of wedding dresses. I've branched out a bit from the standard formula and now sometimes include specific bits of historical detail, about Vichy France, for example, or the early years of Pol Pot.

The other people in the office are quite nice to me, and even though I don't want this to matter, it turns out that it does.

After a while I think they have must have all forgotten about that time in the editorial meeting when I pitched the article about the wedding ring being a piece of bondage equipment.

It turns out I am wrong about that. But it also turns out that it doesn't really matter.

Someone mentions it during some after-work drinks and everybody laughs quite a lot, including me.

Later that night, the woman who mentioned it and made everyone laugh kisses me outside the pub. Her tongue is wet and warm and I am extremely happy that it is in my mouth.

I ask her if she'd like to come home with me but she says no and in some ways that also makes me extremely happy.

I ask her if we should go for a drink this weekend instead and she says yes as long as we don't have to talk too much because the last person she went for a drink with kept talking about getting a loft extension so she continually pretended to mix up patios and lofts just to annoy him.

When she says that I wonder what it might be like to share some things with someone else, perhaps some boredom or some sadness or some utility bills or some blueberries.

When we meet I tell her I am not capable of joy.

She says that she is also not capable of joy.

I wonder how this all looks, me, not yet brave enough to shave my head, not yet brave enough to wear flamboyant clothes that might get mistaken for a costume.

Me, not yet brave enough to feel joy.

⧗

This time is not like all the other times.

If you hurt yourself enough then eventually your body gets the message and something bad starts growing inside you.

There's a whole language for it, and when the time comes, I use it even though I told myself I wouldn't.

She *does* look small, her skin *does* look like paper, I *do* ask her to squeeze my hand if she can hear me.

Also, I'd never knowingly used the word *fitful* before, but when you are watching your mom die, it turns out you can't fucking stop saying it.

I tell three nurses in a row that my mom's breathing is fitful. Or still fitful. Or getting more fitful. I say the word fitful so often that I lose track.

I don't want her to stop breathing.

The third nurse is the kindest, or maybe she just has the most time to be kind.

I ask her if my mom will go that night and she tells me that she can't know for sure but that it will be sometime soon.

She tells me that my mom is comfortable. And I am happy that she tells me this even though I know it is not true.

I know it is not true because the breathing is getting more fitful and also because I am not sure my mom has ever been comfortable in her life. Not even for a minute.

I tell the third nurse this and she nods and tells me that either way it will be soon.

I want to tell her more things about my mom, but I can't remember any of the funny things she used to say.

She was a really funny person, but I can't remember any of the funny things she used to say . . .

Except that whenever she turned off a radiator, she'd sing this weird little song . . .

First the radiator, it gets cold! Then the room and the house get cold! And then we know that the summer is here!

The third nurse smiles, even though that song is not funny at all, and even though I couldn't quite think of the right tune.

⋈

We bury my mom in the ground. Presumably forever.

I book the earliest slot available because it is the cheapest and that is all that I can afford.

The person in the booking office tells me that it used to be called *the pauper's window* and I feel a bit ashamed and then I feel a bit angry that I feel a bit ashamed.

I always thought I would be the strong, silent type at my mom's funeral, but I got that extremely wrong.

I am full of a type of oily guilt and it makes me do strange things all day.

Firstly, I keep rubbing my face up and down the smooth wood of the casket and asking my mom what I am supposed to do and whether my face looks like the face of someone who is utterly scattered and defeated.

Because I feel utterly scattered and defeated, Mom!

At the wake, I stand up on a chair and give a long speech which I am later told focused mainly on the futility of war.

I stand up on a chair again and sing "Danny Boy," which is a song I only know half of the words to.

And then I stand up on a chair again and sing "Close the Coalhouse Door," which is a song I know considerably fewer than half of the words to.

At the end of the night, I take all of the bar receipts out of my trouser pocket, tear them to pieces and start throwing them at people as if they were confetti.

When the bar manager complains about me throwing the receipts, I tell him it is confetti and when he disagrees I tell him that I work at a wedding magazine so I know confetti when I see it.

When sleep finally comes I dream of my mom and she is a marsh bird that sits on my lip and digs at my gums like she is starving.

I get angry and then crush the bird in my fist and stuff the broken bits of wing into the nearest bin.

The next day, the girl who is also not capable of joy comes to my house and wakes me by wiping bits of crust from the corner of my mouth with a baby wipe.

As if I am a fucking baby with diseased gums.

As if I am.

⏳

I have reached a happy medium when it comes to walking.

I still walk sometimes, which is probably a good thing, all things considered, but I have limited the walking to about an hour a day.

Mostly I just walk to the office, no more pools of blood in my socks and, over the course of a few months, every single one of my toenails grows back.

Autumn does what it should, cold and dry and reminding you that at some point you are going to die.

Autumn is the season when you find yourself looking up from your ten toenails and realising whole years of your life have passed.

And for a while this is just the pattern of things, seasons passing, everything being mostly O.K. other than in those moments when everything is utterly terrifying.

I get on a train and it takes me to the sea. Every time I do it, I end up full of you, remembering your strange stories about growing up on an island.

But this time it feels different.

I think about the end of things and that blank space that came before you left.

For the first time I remember how desperate and pathetic I had become and how much you must have hated me.

I picture your angry, sad face and it feels like a thousand fine threads are breaking all at once and lodging themselves in my lungs.

I cough and choke on the thousand fine threads until something begins to move in my lungs and until the sea and the rain blend together in a way that makes the land feel like it is disappearing.

Something is clotting, and that is good.

The air feels tight and heavy and maybe God is with me after all, sorting out the clotting.

I am very, very hungry, I know that.

And I have wasted love, I know that too.

Gradually, gradually, there is someone else. And it turns out that they are capable of joy, after all.

Someone who likes biting the bottom of my ear, for some reason, and whose body is all bones but in a way that never seems bloodless.

Someone who asks why I don't like to go on long walks and when I reply and tell her about the time I spent talking to the birds and how all of my toenails fell off, laughs at me in a way that makes me feel a bit less ridiculous.

And when I tell her about how I have wasted love and how you have grown a whole human being in your body and how I wonder what it looks like, doesn't laugh at me at all.

I start to come to the conclusion that it is O.K. to do nothing, and that maybe I don't have to write a bestselling book about how shit cars are.

Maybe it's just O.K. to do nothing, not because I buried my mom in a cheap plywood box, or because I have wasted love, but just because it turns out that the nothing is actually the something of a life.

I worry that one wrong word might end up knocking us off the highwire but mostly things are fine, and fine things are good things.

A sort of Zeno-skulk, halving the distance between us all the time but never fully coming together, which was also a fine thing and a good thing.

There are still nights when I try to return to you. Nights when I try to think my way back to the copper taste of your skin. But they are rarer now.

The times I do make it back you are always curled up in bed, the way wet soap arcs around a palm.

And these days you never have the head of a fish in my dreams, you just have a normal head.

And these days my head is never a rusty harpoon in my dreams, I also just have a normal head.

Sometimes I have a desire to tie bits of string really tightly around my fingers, but I don't do it.

And sometimes I want to write to you and thank you for making me an animal that actively expects to live.

But I don't do that either.

⋈

For most of the hours in most of the days, I can mostly almost forget you.

But there are still times when the past seems to fold itself into my pocket or into my hands or into the patterns of some brick-work or into the shape of something or other that happens to be near me.

Oh, and also . . . I miss my mom.

I'm a grown up, balding, fat man, and I can't accept that I buried my mom in the ground in a cheap wooden box.

I really miss my mom.

There was this one time, when I was about ten years old. I was eating a bacon sandwich that had been cut up into quarters.

I had saved the biggest quarter, the quarter that seemed like it had the most bacon on it, until last.

But just before I ate it, my mom reached over my shoulder, grabbed it off the plate and shoved it in her mouth.

When she had finished chewing she said:

That will teach you not to save good things until last, never do that, eat the good things first or some cunt like me will come and take them.

I have another memory of her from around the same time.

As a birthday present she had taken me and my best friend to McDonald's and got us each a cheeseburger.

I remember thinking it was the best thing I had ever tasted. And I also remember my mom taking a bite out of it.

When I complained, she took a bite out of my friend's burger too, to even things up, she said.

But the bite she took out of his was bigger than the one she took out of mine.

So to even things up again, she took another small bite out of mine and then declared that everything was now fair and above board.

It took me twenty years to realise that she had only done that because she was hungry too and we could only afford two burgers.

I'm not sure why all my memories of her are about food, but I think it probably has something to do with why I often eat until I am sick and sometimes spend weeks eating nothing but apples and bran flakes.

And why I prefer to eat on my own, and why whenever I eat everything feels a bit quieter and a bit more O.K.

⧗

I have started writing again, mostly because I've got it into my head that I might have something to say about the internet.

Social Media Feudalism: The Land Is Enclosed and You Are the Peasant! (3,208 words)

IRL and BRB No Longer Make Sense! There Is No RL So Where Would You Be RB from? (809 words)

You Know How You Can Block Out the Sun with Your Thumb if You Position It Correctly? Well, That's a Bit Like the Internet, in a Way! (205 words)

And because I have started to laugh again, every now and then, I keep talking about laughing and how nice it is and how maybe I was wrong about it being O.K. to do nothing and how maybe I should write a whole book about laughing.

It starts off O.K.

Book about laughing—draft intro:

Laughing is extremely nice. And we laugh because we are relieved.

We are relieved whenever we move from a state of not knowing a punchline into the state of revealed knowledge that occurs when a punchline is finally uttered.

We are also relieved when we see an object being worked on by gravity. When the waiter drops the plates, we are relieved that maybe the world is as unordered, absurd and chaotic as we suspected it to be all along.

But I run out of things to say quite quickly, and just start writing barely connected things about laughing.

The scientific study of laughter is known as gelotology.

Gelastic syncope is a surprisingly common occurrence—in 2010 there were 207 people worldwide who laughed themselves to death.

In the third century BC, stoic philosopher Chrysippus laughed himself to death after getting his donkey drunk on wine.

I know if I showed this to you, you would say that I don't have to write about everything that is happening to me, and that I don't have to talk about everything that is happening to me either.

⧗

There are always new wedding dresses to describe.

If the market really is an instrument for delivering human desire then this job has taught me that perhaps above all else what humans desire is an extremely large variety of wedding dresses.

Because there are always new wedding dresses to describe, I stay late at work to describe them.

And sometimes, even after I have described all of the wedding dresses that need to be described, I just stay in the office for a bit on my own.

I'll play some music on my computer and watch people moving about in the streets beneath the window.

I'll play slow, wordless music and it makes it seem like the people are dancing a type of ungainly ballet.

Occasionally I find this very moving.

Time has passed and the weather has got cold again.

I am unreasonably calm. As if nothing bad is going to happen. As if my life might just carry on quite painlessly.

This is a new feeling. For most of my life I was sure that bad things were always just about to happen.

Sometimes, when I have stayed late to watch the people and play the music from my computer, I will drink from a hip flask I keep in my backpack.

If I drink enough I'll play a game where I change the music and watch the difference it makes to how the people seem to move in the street.

My eyes always find the people who match the song, so no matter what song I play, it always seems like the world is dancing in time.

On those type of evenings I think that God might finally be with me again. The tardy prick.

When I eventually turn off the computer and head down the stairs, I occasionally panic that when I open the door to the street everybody will be dead.

But deep down, I know they probably aren't.

Something is happening to the mornings. And to the morning light in particular.

For the first time in my life the light seems to arrive gradually, gently, as if a pervert is lightly stroking my nose with some clothing while I sleep.

For my whole life it has always arrived all at once, brutally, as if a pervert is firmly hitting my nose with a shoe while I sleep.

The girl who it turns out can actually bring joy tells me that she is unhappy and that she has slept with someone else.

I tell her that I don't mind that she has slept with someone else because that doesn't really matter.

But she insists that it matters and then insists on leaving.

Before she leaves she tells me that she finds me disgusting because I sometimes (once!) drink wine from a bowl and that living with me is like living with the sad ghost of a failed comedian.

I am not entirely surprised. I had known that the tide was ebbing. But because it was a tide I thought that it would come back in, because that is what tides are supposed to do.

But it didn't come back in. So that's that.

The good thing is that this breakup doesn't turn unhygienic. When you left there were years of mess and gore, of blood and snot and semen and lost toenails.

But this time I continue to do things like make coffee and answer the doorbell and wash my face.

Maybe it really is fine.

I play records and spend a few minutes with the volume down, just watching the grooves of the record silently turning and wondering if they might look a bit like rivers.

And then I turn the volume up and stop thinking about rivers.

Unless the song is about rivers, or reminds me of rivers.

Sometimes I sing so much that my tongue ends up feeling like something dry that I need to spit out.

I finally summon the bravery to shave my head. It is an O.K. shape. Which is a fucking relief.

There's a slight bump on the back, enough that when I rub it, it reminds me of your handwriting.

I rub it quite a lot when I write.

Erotic Monodirectionality: You Cannot Love Something Against Its Will (28,234 words)

You write to me again. Just like before, I know it is from you as soon as I see the envelope.

I wonder if I might have summoned the letter by continually rubbing the weird bump on my head.

I still sort of think that type of magic is real and that I was probably born with some sort of natural flair for it.

Like the last time you wrote, it takes me days to open the letter.

I get it into my head that it might be a letter full of bad news. Maybe you have written to tell me that you have cracked a rib or lost an eye or become a libertarian.

But it doesn't say that. The letter says that you will be in the city for a few weeks and that if I am around, and would like to, it would be nice to catch up after all this time.

It doesn't seem to me like a lot of time has passed, but I text the number written at the bottom of the page and say I am free pretty much every single day.

It isn't the same café as the first time, but it feels like it.

It sells miniature bottles of wine and standard bottles of beer.

I am there early and I sit peeling the label off one of the tiny bottles of white wine.

You sit down and make a joke about how old we both look.

I speak too much.

You don't look old at all! I know I do though, I've fallen to bits and then come back together again quite a few times and I think that ages you! Ha!

Honestly, though, it could be worse, for a while there I just looked like cold, white, uncooked meat! Ha!

I settle down eventually and manage to gulp down the words that keep lodging in my cheeks . . . words like *doom* and *curse* and *prophecy* and *hex*.

I try to say empty, simple words.

You look the same.

Hair you could read like runes, splayed over your shoulder like a paintbrush.

Hand like a carving of a thin, brown bird.

It feels like expecting and remembering all at once.

I try to say empty, simple words.

⋈

I try to tell you that I am sorry, and say things like . . . *Christ, we were so fucking young!*

But you sense it coming and stop me.

Because you are still kind.

When you ask how I have been I tell you that things have been O.K. and that people have been kind to me and some people have even loved me and that mostly I have been happy.

But I leave out quite a lot. I leave out the bleeding feet and the talking to the birds and the time the masturbating Russian man watched me cry next to his naked ex-wife and I miss out the time I pulled myself around on my stomach and it left angry welts.

That's the type of thing I leave out.

I don't leave out my job describing wedding dresses or how I felt ashamed having to bury my mom really early in the morning because it was cheap and I don't leave out the story of shouting at the child in the supermarket because I thought he was stealing my beans.

Although as soon as I say it, I wish I had left out the weeping child bean-theft story.

I tell you I am thinking of leaving the city and living nearer the sea. Which isn't really true, but feels true when I say it.

You ask whether I ever finished the book about how cars are shit. I tell you that I haven't but that I might write a book about the internet or a book about laughing instead.

I realise how much I have wanted to talk to you, and how much I have wanted to hear you talk back to me and how much I have wanted to see your mouth move while you do it.

The sun shutters up your face, and my chest pulses like a broken bell and I know God is there.

When there is a silence I feel the urge to tell you that I am dying.

I don't know why, but I keep wanting to tell you that I am dying, even though I'm not dying at all, or not in anything other than the broadest possible way . . .

When I tell you that, you laugh. And when you laugh it is like a thick wave of white silk unfurls from your throat and settles on the table between us.

For a second it feels like it is that first morning again. That first morning with its first light.

But it is not that morning and it is not that light.

⋈

You tell me your child's name.

And he has a really, really great name.

You show me a picture of your child.

And he is the most beautiful thing I have ever seen.

Not the most beautiful person I have ever seen, the most beautiful thing.

Which is a much bigger category, I say.

I know it is, you say.

⧖

I always think there is more that needs to be said, even when there is nothing more that needs to be said and when what actually needs to happen is that people need to go home.

There's the bit just before you leave when I realise that I used to always tell you that I wish I had known you when you were young, even just for a day, just to see what you were like.

But that now I wish that I could know you when you are old, even just for a day, just to see what you are like.

And then there's the bit when you actually do leave.

I think it will feel like we are the final pair left on the dance-floor after the lights have come up, but it doesn't feel like that.

Or that it will feel like we are singing a hymn in a really old building with no roof, but it doesn't feel like that either.

Or it will feel like it is O.K. to string our veins to the stars and like it is O.K. to love that we love what we love.

But it isn't like that. Not really.

Because there isn't a bit after the bit where you actually do leave.

Because there is no after. After never comes.

After has always been there. After is always there. Always turning away.

ACKNOWLEDGEMENTS

This book was made possible by the collective support, patience and love shown to me by so many people. I'm grateful. And I'm lucky. Special thanks go to my agent, Clare Conville, and the wider C&W team for their consistent belief in the book, and in me. And also to Anna Kelly and all at Little, Brown and Hachette. Being edited by Anna has been a genuine gift; whatever this book is, it is because of her brilliance and her care. And thank you also to the entire team at Europa Editions. Thank you to all of my friends (Delinquents and former Delinquents in particular) for putting up with me. I love you all very much. And lastly to my family, and to Olivia, for well, you know . . . everything.

NOTE

At various points in this book, the narrator makes reference or indirect allusion to the words or ideas of the following authors. "Architecture is the art that works most slowly but most surely on the human soul!" is a version of "Architecture, of all the arts, is the one which acts the most slowly, but the most surely, on the soul," from *The Art of Thinking*, by Ernest Dimnet. "Habit is the ballast that chains the dog to its vomit!" is a reference to the line in *Proust*, by Samuel Beckett. "Art thanks existence by honouring that which prefigures utopia" is a fragment from a letter by Theodor W. Adorno which appears in *Grand Hotel Abyss: The Lives of the Frankfurt School*, by Stuart Jeffries. "If the revolution doesn't have dancing that is disguised as throwing bricks but is actually just dancing, then it isn't my revolution!" is a reference to the Emma Goldman quote "If I can't dance, I don't want to be in your revolution." Ideas about the birth of recorded sound and vibrato on page 153 were inspired by the history of recording techniques in *The Rest Is Noise* by Alex Ross.

The image of economics as palm reading and of the relationship between kink and monogamy were partly inspired by the work of Conner Habib. The passage on page 186 was based on a story Habib told about his mother on a June 2017 episode of the podcast Unregistered with Thaddeus Russell, which chimed with the author's own childhood.

ABOUT THE AUTHOR

Keiran Goddard is the author of one poetry pamphlet (*Strings*) and two full-length poetry collections, *For the Chorus* and *Votive*, the first of which was shortlisted for the Melita Hume Prize and runner-up for the William Blake Prize.

He speaks on issues related to social change and currently develops research on workers' rights, the future of work, automation, and trade unionism. *Hourglass* is his debut novel.